TERROR IN THE WOODS

Dave walked slowly toward the campsite, straining for a glimpse of one of the others. "All right, you guys, play your silly games."

Still no answer. The camp was silent. "C'mon, you guys! You're pissing me off."

Dave approached the grill, then stood looking foolishly about. Where were they? Fear gripped him again. A flickering kerosene lamp at one end of the table seemed to beckon to him. Without knowing why, he moved toward it, picked it up, and slowly made his way toward the edge of the woods.

With each new step, he paused to listen. He wasn't sure what he expected. Hearing nothing, he continued to move forward.

A snapping sound made Dave whirl around, but it was too late. A bullwhip had caught him around the neck and jerked him off his feet.

The last thing he saw was a glint of steel from the rapier-sharp blade that sliced across his throat.

PINNACLE BOOKS HAS
SOMETHING FOR EVERYONE —

MAGICIANS, EXPLORERS, WITCHES AND CATS

THE HANDYMAN (377-3, $3.95/$4.95)
He is a magician who likes hands. He likes their comfortable shape and weight and size. He likes the portability of the hands once they are severed from the rest of the ponderous body. Detective Lanark must discover who The Handyman is before more handless bodies appear.

PASSAGE TO EDEN (538-5, $4.95/$5.95)
Set in a world of prehistoric beauty, here is the epic story of a courageous seafarer whose wanderings lead him to the ends of the old world — and to the discovery of a new world in the rugged, untamed wilderness of northwestern America.

BLACK BODY (505-9, $5.95/$6.95)
An extraordinary chronicle, this is the diary of a witch, a journal of the secrets of her race kept in return for not being burned for her "sin." It is the story of Alba, that rarest of creatures, a white witch: beautiful and able to walk in the human world undetected.

THE WHITE PUMA (532-6, $4.95/NCR)
The white puma has recognized the men who deprived him of his family. Now, like other predators before him, he has become a man-hater. This story is a fitting tribute to this magnificent animal that stands for all living creatures that have become, through man's carelessness, close to disappearing forever from the face of the earth.

*For dear Edie & Bill —
Thanks for listening
while this was aborning.
Much love to you both,
Mary Lee and Rob**

THE KEEPER
ROBERT D. LEE

A.K.A. Robert D. Lee

PINNACLE BOOKS
WINDSOR PUBLISHING CORP.

PINNACLE BOOKS are published by

Windsor Publishing Corp.
475 Park Avenue South
New York, NY 10016

First Printing: June, 1993
Printed in the United States of America

Prologue

It was feeding time and the cats were hungry. He had to hurry. If the cats were upset, they did not perform well.

He had removed a side of meat from the locker earlier in the day to give it time to thaw. It now lay on its side on the large butcher block, razor-sharp cutting instruments lined up like surgeon's tools directly beside it. Buckets were carefully placed on the floor below to catch the flow of blood.

With a long, slender knife, he made an incision around the hip joint. Then, with a flatter and sturdier blade, he separated the lips of the wound, cutting away at muscle and tendon. Rivulets of fresh blood coursed along the table and dripped into the bucket right next to his foot.

He gave the bone a sharp twist but could not wrest it from its socket. Some animals were like that, he thought. Stubborn to the end. Even in death.

With a mighty smash, he brought the heavy cleaver down and split the joint in two. The leg bounced, then slithered toward the edge of the table.

His blood-stained hand thrust forward and snatched it back. Sweat glistened on his brow and he brushed it away, leaving a trail of red across his forehead and down the side of his nose.

He did not like this task at all. The sound of cracking bones, the coppery stench of blood, and the slippery sensation of animal muscle converged in a single, overwhelming response that made him physically ill. Nevertheless, he went on.

There it was again. The muted cry was louder now. The cats were restless. He feared one of them was about to die.

There was something pitiful about the newest member of the group. Clearly, it wasn't as strong as the others and he knew it could hardly survive the rigorous training it was about to undergo. He sighed with resignation, knowing only too well that if this one could not live up to the standard of performance expected of it, he'd be forced to butcher it and feed it to the others.

The steady accumulation of animals now caged in the cavernous cellar of the vast stone mansion had grown to a number he could scarcely handle. Time after time, he had been tempted to release them all, perhaps even escape himself; but in the end, he could never find the strength to do it.

That was always the problem, wasn't it, he thought. Someone was always telling him what to do, whether he wanted to do it or not.

One

From the moment they entered the woods early that morning, someone had been following them.

They had set up camp the way they always did, this time selecting a site at the edge of the woods, a short distance from a field of wild strawberries they'd spotted on a hike through this same area the week before.

It was Kathy Kraus who insisted they return. The spot had everything they needed in a campsite, with the added advantage of being so close to home. No one knew where they were. They were just as isolated as they would have been with a five-hour drive further upstate. The place was perfect as far as Kathy was concerned.

The two couples had camped together so frequently, setting up the site had become routine. Each of them had an assigned chore and performed it with no questions asked. Air mattresses were filled and holes dug to place the tent poles within minutes of arrival.

Dave Carter was the tent expert. He slipped the

rings over the poles, set them into the holes he had dug moments before, and pulled the tarp taut. Then, he did the same for the other tent that was lying in a collapsed heap a few feet away. "Beat Dave's Clock" was a game he liked to play with himself whenever he set up camp. This particular morning, he managed to shave two minutes off his previous record.

At twenty-four, his reddish baby-fine hair had already started to thin. Translated, this meant plenty of sunblock on camping trips to prevent a painfully scorched scalp at the end of the day. Lean and hard-muscled, he had the kind of body that required constant cinching at the waistline. Otherwise, shorts, trousers, or any garment covering his private parts would slip past his hips and down around his ankles.

Dave turned to the others, a self-satisfied smirk on his freckled face. "If the ladies ever get it together, Ron and I would be pleased to have them join us for a little swim before lunch."

Kathy looked up from the cooler where she was foraging among the tightly packed foodstuffs, trying to find enough space for one more six-pack of beer. She was what people called "pleasant looking," with thick blonde hair that hung halfway down her back when it wasn't secured with a rubber band or caught in a single braid as it was now. Intent blue eyes studied the multiple configurations she created. Then came a sigh of resignation.

"Take this down to the river and keep it cold," she instructed, handing Dave the six-pack. "I think we brought too much beer."

As he dragged an air mattress toward one of the tents, Ron Richards stopped in his tracks. "Give me a break!" he laughed. "There's no such thing as too much beer. I'll kill that baby myself long before lunch."

Truthfully speaking, Ron wasn't much interested in beer, swimming, or in lunch. At least not for the moment. Camping made him horny. There wasn't a lot he liked better than "doing it" in the woods. It was all he had been able to think about all week long.

Once, when he was a kid, on a beautiful spring afternoon, he had come out of the family garage and heard the grown-ups laughing. His mother had missed the point or didn't hear what was said, so his father had to repeat it. To this day, Ron could still see his dad, next to the barbecue grill, fork in hand, pointed upward to the sky, as he recited, "Hooray, hooray, it's the first of May! Outdoor fucking begins today."

The grown-ups all laughed again, but Ron thought it was the most exciting thing he ever heard. Then and there, he made himself a solemn promise to honor that date as often as he could, once he got a little older and could find himself a willing partner.

The partner showed up on the day Ron met Melissa Galvin. He found himself staring into a face with a perky little nose and deep dark eyes, fringed with gold-tipped lashes. Uncontrollable ringlets of shining brown hair framed an Irish complexion that was flawless. But more at issue were the long, graceful legs, compact buttocks, tiny waist, and full, shapely breasts. Just looking at her caused a

9

hot, insistent rush to his loins.

Ron still had the muscular physique of the wily quarterback he'd been in high school. He was wide-shouldered and deep-chested and with dark good looks that elected him "Most Handsome" in his graduating class.

As luck would have it, Melissa lusted after Ron with the same passion he felt for her. This was the final Saturday in August, and together they had honored Ron's boyhood commitment on every weekend camping trip the foursome made that summer.

Still clutching the six-pack, Dave watched as Ron shoved the air mattress inside the tent. Melissa followed behind.

"Come on, you two," he yelled after them. "It's too early for that stuff."

Ron poked his head out of the tent. "It's never too early," he grinned.

"I'm going down to the river. Are you coming or not?" With that, he strode out of the clearing and into the woods.

A sheepish Ron appeared at the tent flap. "Okay, okay, I'm coming," he yelled, pulling on his bathing suit, and hurried after him.

Moments later, while Kathy and Melissa set up the folding table they'd later use for supper, she couldn't ignore the eager look in Melissa's eye. They spread an oilcloth cover over the table and smoothed it flat.

"You're very lucky," Kathy stated, without ever looking straight at Melissa. "I wish Dave were a little more like Ron."

Melissa said nothing, just smiled a secret little smile, picked up a hamper of sandwiches, and headed toward the edge of the woods.

Kathy took a final look around to make sure everything was in place, then followed. Melissa was already halfway down the wooded slope leading to the river when Kathy finally caught up with her. She watched the firm, shapely buttocks rise and fall beneath Melissa's shorts as she picked her way down the rock-strewn path. The lean hard body in front of her was a clear reminder of what hers was not.

Kathy was large and slightly overweight, but it had never bothered her before, not until this summer when she and Dave had begun the weekend ritual of camping with Melissa and Ron.

At some point, usually not long after the campsite was ready, Melissa could be counted on to shuck her clothes and prance about in the nude.

It was something Kathy couldn't bring herself to do. Not that she was a prude or anything like that; but running around with her large breasts flying and her ample rump jiggling up and down wasn't exactly the way she wanted to present herself to Dave, whose sexual energies weren't always reliable, at best.

What she really preferred was to steal away into their tent and make love to him within the downy comfort of their sleeping bag. Failing that, she was very happy to search for a scenic and comfortable spot where they could read some poetry together before it got too dark. There weren't many young men in the town where she was raised who ever read

11

poetry unless it had been forced on them in high school English class. Dave was definitely an exception. But then, Dave had also gone to school twenty-five miles away.

By the time Kathy and Melissa reached the river-bank, Dave was already swimming several feet from shore. Ron stood ankle-deep in water.

Moments later, Melissa had stripped down to a thong bikini and was leaping toward him through the shallow water, laughing and screeching as she ran.

Close by, a solitary figure squatted in a thicket of bushes running along the bank of the river. Not a muscle moved to betray his presence.

Shrieks of high hilarity echoed through the river-bed. The couple frolicked in the water, splashing at each other as they moved toward a bend where the river twisted, turned, then disappeared from sight.

Their gleeful sounds sparked a flame of rage that was smoldering within him.

He rose, and for a brief moment recklessly abandoned his cover. Seconds later, dashing from tree to tree, he was able to keep them in view without being seen himself. The muscles in his face began to twitch.

Finally, he moved closer to the river where he knelt in deep grass and peered cautiously through the tall blades. His eyes burned in disbelief.

He had lost sight of them. But it would not be for long.

* * *

Melissa screamed with delight as Ron wrestled her into deeper water and ripped off the last, tiny piece of clothing that separated her from complete nudity. This done, he waved it triumphantly in the air and put it on his head. They both howled at the absurdity of the picture he made, then moments later they were locked in a lustful and watery embrace. Ron's arms floated on the surface of the river, encircling Melissa's body. Then he began a slow, rhythmic breaststroke, gradually pushing her forward with his chest, as they headed for a bend in the river. Soon they were completely out of sight.

"Think they'll make it back to camp by suppertime?" Dave inquired, a sly grin curling at one corner of his mouth.

"Depends on the mosquitoes," Kathy responded. "If they're really biting, they'll be back before lunch." Dave laughed and swam toward shore where the six-pack lay nestled among a clump of stones. He waded toward it and Kathy took an appreciative look at the way his wet undershorts clung to his body. *My God,* she thought, *he's been swimming in this cold river and he's got an erection!* This sort of arousal wasn't Dave's usual style, but she decided not to comment.

He wrestled a can of beer from its plastic collar, popped the metallic ring at the top, and extended it in Kathy's direction.

"Thirsty?"

As Kathy reached out to take it from him, Dave placed his hand over hers. They locked eyes, each with a clear reading of the other's thoughts.

"C'mon, Kath," he pleaded. "No one'll see us. It won't be like last time, I promise."

"I'm not thinking about last time," she insisted. "I'm just not all that keen to roll around in the dirt."

"It doesn't seem to bother Melissa any."

"I'm not Melissa. And you know it."

"Then let's put it this way. I'm embarrassed. I want a chance to try it again. A guy loses his hard-on, he loses confidence."

"Maybe if you'd been with Melissa, it wouldn't have happened."

"Don't start with that again. If you ask me she's too skinny. I like a woman with some meat on her bones."

Kathy laughed, in spite of herself. "Well, you've sure got that, all right!"

His brown eyes were deep and earnest. When he looked like that, her resolve turned to mush. She couldn't deny him anything. Besides, if the place didn't suit her, Dave certainly did. And if making love in broad daylight turned him on, she wasn't about to turn him down. Other than Melissa and Ron, she felt sure there wasn't another living soul for miles around.

At the river's edge was a long flat rock, concealed for the most part by a clump of bushes that nearly surrounded it. Dave led her toward it by the hand.

Together they stretched out naked, warmed by the afternoon sun.

No words were exchanged between them. From

time to time, only a low moan broke the silence of the afternoon.

Dave leaned toward her and ran his tongue along the side of her neck. His nostrils filled with the sweet smell of her sunbaked skin. Gently, he drew her toward him and placed his hands under her buttocks. He didn't intend for it to happen this fast; but within seconds, he felt himself deep within her.

He swallowed convulsively. His breath came in short gasps. Slowly, she rolled beneath him, like a skiff tossed by the insistent roll of the incoming tide. Back and forth she moved, oblivious to the stone slab that made their bed. Her hips thrust toward him, then lowered, again and again, faster and faster, when suddenly and without warning the explosion came.

For a moment, she was blinded by its power. She cried aloud, then laughed; but Dave scarcely noticed. His own movements had doubled in speed and ferocity until he, too, cried out. He sucked air back into his lungs, like a drowning man, then collapsed in a limp heap on top of her.

They lay perfectly still and motionless, each fully aware that something very special had just occurred between them.

It was Kathy who broke the silence. "Dave . . ."

"Mmmmm," he responded.

"Mmmmm," she replied. Then, after a long moment, "Dave, we're gonna be okay."

From a ledge on the slope above them, the shadowy figure lay hidden. The stalker had climbed to a rocky promontory high above the river. This way, he could keep an eye on all of them.

Below, the chubby girl and her boyfriend were making love. It disgusted him but he'd take care of them later.

It was the dark one he wanted. Earlier, he watched as she ran through the woods like a sleek, young panther and promised himself he wouldn't let this one get away.

His breath was coming in short gasps. From his secret place among the rocks, he raised his head and looked around. There was a splashing in the river down below.

Again, the muscles in his face began to twitch. Rolling over on his back, he withdrew a knife from the sheath on his belt. It glinted off a ray of sunlight streaking through the trees. With a soft murmur, tenderly he caressed its blade.

When Kathy and Dave awoke, the sun had already dropped behind the trees that lined the edge of the slope above them. They stared back at one another sleepily and smiled.

"I'm saving the next one for tonight," Dave grinned.

"Just don't forget where you left off," Kathy smiled back.

When he was on his feet, she watched him pull on the soggy jockey shorts he'd shucked so fast a couple of hours before. Dave was reed-thin and probably weighed the same as he did in high school, Kathy thought. If she and Dave decided to get married, she promised herself to lose twenty pounds before the wedding. That settled, she wiggled back into her shorts and tee shirt.

"Do you think they've finished yet?" she asked, wondering when they might expect to see Melissa and Ron.

"Probably not," Dave laughed. "Let's go back to camp without them. I'll get the barbecue ready so we can eat early tonight. Looks to me like everybody forgot about lunch!"

They walked in silence for a bit, then climbed the rocky path from the river that led up to the campsite. When they stopped for a moment to catch their breath, a squirrel leaped from branch to branch in a tree just in front of them.

They had shucked their clothes and left them lying on the riverbank to be retrieved on their way back to the campsite. Melissa and Ron made their way back upstream, retrieved the abandoned items, and picked their way through the woods.

Deeper in the woods, the stalker followed. Only now, he was close enough to hear their conversation.

They paused for a final embrace before reaching camp, when suddenly, Melissa wrenched herself free and spun about in alarm.

"What was that?" she whispered hoarsely.

"What was what?" Ron wasn't really interested. He was more intent on another quickie before they left the woods.

"I saw someone," she insisted.

"Don't be crazy," he laughed. "There's nobody here but us rabbits."

"I'm not kidding, Ron." Melissa was frightened, and the fact that he had another erection wasn't going to change her mind. "There's someone hiding behind those trees."

"Honey, I promise you. There's nobody for miles around."

Melissa wasn't buying. Frozen with fear, unable to move, she grabbed his wrist, her lacquered fingernails digging at his flesh.

"I'll prove it to you, okay?" he grinned. "You think you saw someone? Where?"

Wordlessly, she pointed to a dense growth of bushes a short distance from the path. Ron pounded his chest like King Kong, then moved in the direction of her pointing finger. "Come out, come out, whoever you are!" he shouted at the bushes, cupping his hands around his mouth. He ran forward, arms extended to either side as if to block the escape of anyone who might suddenly burst forth. He then turned and smiled at Melissa. "What did I tell you?"

She stood, still riveted to the spot. Ron was clowning around and she was terrified.

"Hey, you!" he called, parting the branches in front of him. "If you've been watching, I hope you enjoyed the show. Today was one of my better performances." With that, he grabbed himself around the neck with one hand and hopped backward into the underbrush until he was completely hidden from view.

"Okay, you win," Melissa yelled after him. Maybe she was wrong. Now, all she wanted was to get back to camp. Fast.

The bushes rustled. Suddenly, she was frightened again. "Ron," she called tentatively, not sure what she expected. He didn't answer. "Ron, this isn't funny. Come out of there," she ordered.

Nothing.

Without thinking, she ran off the path into the woods, shouting Ron's name. Melissa was still too distant from the campsite for anyone to hear her scream.

Once they reached the campsite, Kathy busied herself at the picnic table they'd set up earlier for the evening meal. This was one of the camping rituals she thoroughly enjoyed. The plates they used were merely cardboard, but the foursome made a point of serving their predinner drinks in real glassware. Kathy had bought a set of stemmed glasses specifically for this occasion.

Carefully, she wiped each of them with a paper towel, assuring herself that no dust or dirt remained that might have settled while they were away from camp in the afternoon.

Traditionally, their cocktail hour consisted of a combination of vodka and some kind of juice. Sometimes it was cranberry, sometimes grapefruit. This particular weekend the choice had been orange.

Since Kathy occasionally worked as a waitress or barmaid filling in for her mother at the Stony Creek Rathskeller whenever it was necessary, she was officially proclaimed campsite bartender the first weekend this foursome headed off together into the woods

"You know what would be great?" she asked Dave as she rearranged the glasses and the vodka bottle into a neat configuration at one end of the table. "I'm going to pick some of those strawberries in the field we passed when we came in here. I'll put them in the cooler for a while, then slice them in thin little pieces and float them in our drinks." She looked at Dave, eagerly awaiting his response.

"Honest opinion?" he asked.

Kathy nodded.

"Relax. You work too hard. Learn to enjoy yourself."

"But it would be nice, Dave. Don't you think?"

"Sure. But we're supposed to be relaxing. Having fun."

"It's no trouble, honest. I like doing stuff like that. Give me one of those plastic bags in the food box. I'll be back before you know it."

"If those two don't show up by the time the grill is ready, I'm going down there and drag them back by the pubic hair!"

The two tossed their heads back and roared with laughter at the image Dave created.

He began pouring charcoal onto the grill as Kathy disappeared into the woods.

The sun sank lower and lower as Kathy trudged through the strawberry field. Now that she was picking strawberries, she might as well pick enough for dessert and some for the following week, as well. Maybe she should bring some home for her mother as a surprise.

Poor Mom, she thought. She didn't get many pleasant surprises, but she'd sure had her share of unpleasant ones. A woman with no skills and two mouths to feed had to take any job she could find, if there was no husband around to help her. When Trudy Kraus was hired by Ellen Wallace to work as a waitress at the Stony Creek Rathskeller, she thought her prayers had been answered.

For a long while, Kathy sat among the strawberry vines and thought about the afternoon. Kathy never knew her father, but very early in life she promised herself she would never have the life her mother had. Somehow between them, they managed to scrape together enough money to get her through state college and now she was a teacher. She taught second grade in the same school she had gone to as a little girl.

Dave worked in a hardware store his uncle owned thirty miles away. They'd met at the Rathskeller on one of the evenings she'd worked her mother's shift. He wasn't exactly the man she always thought she'd marry; but he sure wasn't the type who'd leave a wife and baby daughter six months after she was born.

Maybe Dave wasn't passionate or the best lover she'd ever had, but he was solid. That counted for a lot. Besides, they'd had very good sex that afternoon. Maybe things were changing for the better. Maybe, at last, her whole life was changing for the better.

Kathy was twenty-three; and in a town like Ruttenburg, at twenty-three, it was high time she got married. Dave wasn't the stud some of the guys in town claimed to be; but who needed them, anyway? A movie once in a while, just to put a good face on things, when all they wanted was a good fuck? That's how her mother wrecked her life.

No, Kathy decided. Her life was going to be different. At first she had wondered if Dave ever intended to sleep with her. Then, when they began these camping weekends together, it all changed, thanks to the undeniable proximity of two people in one sleeping bag.

It was getting late and it was almost dark. Kathy looked at her watch. She'd better hurry.

Back at the campsite, she found Dave was gone. Coals were neatly piled and the barbecue grill was ready to be lit. Dave took no chances, she thought. Ron and Melissa had better be in plain sight before he'd start his fire. Steaks would be placed on the fire at the precise moment the coals were at their hottest. He wouldn't dream of sacrificing the moment because two of their foursome were busy elsewhere.

Summer dusk was fading rapidly. It was almost completely dark. Kathy lit two kerosene lamps and set them on the picnic table. She began to wonder if Dave had remembered to bring a flashlight with him. At this hour of the evening, she had no choice.

At the edge of the wood, she fully expected to hear voices as the three picked their way up the rocky incline heading back to camp. Kathy stood quite still and listened. The only sound was the flock of sparrows twittering away at nightfall. A breeze had sprung up off the river and she felt a chill. She moved slowly, following the beam of light in front of her. They had a much-more-powerful lantern back at camp. She began to wish she'd taken that one.

Up ahead, silhouetted trees merged one with the other until they formed what appeared to be an impenetrable curtain of stately black shapes. In the light of early afternoon, following the path had been quite simple. Now it was almost impossible.

Obviously, she'd never find her way to the river with this silly flashlight, she told herself. She'd better go back to camp and get the other one.

Clouds were moving swiftly across the moon; and each time its light was lost, she stood motionless, peering into the darkness.

Without warning, a cold fear gripped her. What if something terrible had happened?

She imagined she heard something. She listened again; but this time, it was only the sound of crickets.

Then she heard it again.

A moaning noise came from a clump of saplings only a few feet away. She hurried in its direction, pushing aside branches of the young trees that stung her face, the beam of light roving back and forth before her as she ran. Up ahead was a tiny clearing among the trees.

The moment she reached it, a scream of terror burst from her lungs.

Melissa was on her knees, both arms tied at the wrists around the trunk of a larger tree. Kathy played her light across her face and down her body. There was a large bruise on her left cheek and one eye was swollen shut. Her lips were puffed and bloodied. She was nearly unconscious, and the only reason she had not slipped to the ground was that she'd been tied so tightly to the tree.

Had Ron Richards suddenly gone berserk? How could they have spent so much time together without knowing there was a sadistic madman in their midst?

Kathy almost screamed again, but someone grabbed her from behind. Her eyes and throat burned from the searing stench of chloroform soaking the rag that covered her face.

In college, she was famous for the miraculous saves she made while tending goal for the women's field hockey team. Wielding that hockey stick, her moves were swift and accurate. Speed and accuracy were all that could save her now. Trying not to inhale the overpowering fumes, she twisted her lower body and slammed her flashlight into the groin of her assailant.

He cried out in pain as he stumbled forward, nearly losing his balance. But he recovered quickly. Desperately, her eyes searched the darkness, hoping for something, anything, to use as a weapon.

She backed away, aiming her flashlight at the ground, anxious to discover a heavy stick or loose rock lying near her feet.

In that instant, the man lunged for her again. Kathy raised the flashlight and flailed at him wildly. He caught her by the wrist and knocked it from her hand. The flashlight fell to the ground with a dull thud and its light went out.

With a viselike grip, he clasped her head between his hands. Frantically, she squirmed, attempting to twist her face, first in one direction and then the other. She heard nothing but the sound of his raspy breathing as she struggled to free herself, but this time she could not break away. Again, her nose and mouth were smothered by the chloroform-soaked rag. There was a loud ringing in her ears and her brain began to spin out of control. Kathy felt her strength begin to ebb. Her knees buckled and darkness enveloped her.

Two

When Dave finally groped his way back to camp, he noticed that the fire had already been started. A wave of relief washed over him.

He hadn't been able to find Ron and Melissa anywhere and he was starting to feel uneasy. He'd shouted and called their names over and over again, but the only voice he heard in response was his own, echoing down the steep banks of the riverbed.

In truth, he'd begun to feel uneasy almost as soon as he left the campsite. It wasn't something he could give a name to, just a weird sense of foreboding, a kind of feeling he didn't often have.

It was stupid. After all, Melissa and Ron had gone off on their own frequently in the past. No questions asked. Then they'd show up at camp while Kathy was mixing up a batch of Sea Breezes in the big mason jar they used for a cocktail shaker. They never explained where they'd been, but there wasn't any need to explain. They all knew what they knew.

But Dave's apprehension began to grow when he discovered a strange patch of ground covered with dead leaves. It was almost completely dark when he stumbled on it and he could hardly see. When he brushed away some of the leaves, he found a network of thin branches woven into what seemed to be a covering for a fairly deep hole.

In the morning, he'd come back again when it was light and have a better look. If this was an animal trap of some kind, it was completely illegal. Everyone was worried about wildlife and the environment these days. If his suspicions proved to be correct, Dave intended to contact his cousin Joe, who was a forest ranger, and report this to him.

What if there were more of these things scattered throughout the woods? He began to worry, cautiously making his way back to camp.

He had a sudden picture of Ron and Melissa innocently cavorting through the woods, then plummeting without warning into unexpected depths below.

The sight of glowing embers on the barbecue grill dispelled his sense of mounting anxiety.

"Hey, Kath!" Dave shouted, trying not to sound too giddy with the relief he was feeling at the moment. "I sure could use one of those orange and vodka things with your little strawberries floating in it!"

He walked slowly toward the campsite, straining for a glimpse of one of the others. "All right, you guys, play your silly game. Jump out and yell 'boo' so we can all have cocktails."

Still no answer. The camp was silent. "C'mon, you guys. You're pissing me off. I'm dry as the Gobi Desert."

Dave approached the grill, then stood looking foolishly about. Had they all gone back to the woods looking for him? This could go on all night, he mused. If he left now and went looking for them, they might return, find him gone, and go out looking again.

No, he decided, it was better to stay put. Soon, they'd all gather in one place. He hoped it would happen before the coals got too cool to put the steaks on. Otherwise, their cooking time would get all screwed up and that infuriated him. Maybe it was time to have a little man-to-man conversation with Ron. If tonight's meal worked out, it would be a miracle.

Where were they? Dave wasn't sure if he was annoyed or if that gnawing fear was beginning to return. What if they had stumbled onto that thing with the dry leaves on top and plunged into some kind of pit?

No, he told himself. If they had, someone would have screamed for help.

Maybe not. Fear gripped him again. A flickering kerosene lamp at one end of the table seemed to beckon to him. Without knowing why, he moved toward it, picked it up, and slowly made his way toward the edge of the woods.

With each new step, he paused to listen. He wasn't sure what he expected. Hearing nothing, he continued to move forward. No. There was something. A tapping sound. A slow, dull tapping. He took several steps, holding the lantern above his head to illuminate the way.

He stopped near a large oak. There it was again, only louder. The same slow, deliberate sound. He held the lantern even higher and looked up.

"Oh, my God!" he cried, jamming his fist between his teeth. "Oh, dear sweet Jesus!"

Ron Richards grinned down at him, suspended by a rope strung beneath both arms. Actually, it was more a grimace than a grin. Ron's throat had been slit clean across below the jaw line, and his body turned slowly from side to side, gently propelled by the breeze of a calm summer night.

A snapping sound made Dave whirl around, but it was too late. A bullwhip had caught him around the neck and jerked him off his feet.

The last thing he saw was a glint of steel from the rapier-sharp blade that sliced across his throat.

Three

It had been dark for hours before he got home. In the bathroom, next to the monklike chamber in which he slept, he stripped off his soiled clothes and turned on the water in the basin. He watched as the steady stream cleansed away the dirt and grime. He took infinite pride in his hands. They were the hands of an artist and few things upset him more than the sight of grit beneath his nails.

He stared at his own reflection in the mirror, studying it as though he had never seen it before. A dull ache began to throb at his temples. He dried his face on an old worn towel, reached behind the bathroom door, and removed his robe from the hook.

He closed his eyes against the pain. Tiny bursts of light were flashing before his eyes and closing them did not make them disappear. The throbbing grew steadily worse. He leaned his head against the bathroom door and began to retch.

It felt as though someone were sticking needles into the corner of his eyeballs, pushing them up into the frontal lobe of his brain. Finally, unable to endure the excruciating pain any longer, he staggered back against the door and collapsed in a heap on the floor.

Hans did not know how long he had lain there. When he came to, he opened his eyes and the headache was gone. He shivered. Perspiration had soaked his robe.

"You make me puke," a voice said, unexpectedly disrupting the silence of the darkened room.

Hans stared unblinkingly. His heart pounded. Maybe if I remain completely still, he won't torture me again. He wants an excuse, but I won't give it to him. I'm on to him now. I'll just sit here very quietly until he goes away.

Then Hans cried out as his head slammed against the wall. Still, he would not speak.

"You don't fool me, you limpid wretch. I can read your thoughts," the voice shrieked at him. "Why do you disobey me?"

"You've gone too far," Hans finally replied, almost inaudibly.

"Too far? I haven't gone far enough! If you weren't such a miserable, cowardly nitwit, you'd see that for yourself."

Hans knew there was no way to win this argument, yet he had to try. "We have more mouths than we can feed. Still, you bring home more."

"Your job is to see that they are fed. I'll worry about their mouths."

"That's just it. You don't. You don't worry about anything."

A peal of laughter rang through the upper corridor of the vast stone mansion. Hans lowered his eyes and stared at the floor.

"Then I have very good news, dear Hans. Soon we may part company forever. Once I find my prize, my Felidia, the act will be complete. The cats will be exquisitely trained and I shall resume where I left off when our dear parents met their tragic end. At last the Von Ziegler name shall be restored to the heights of glory it once enjoyed."

Hans made no reply. In the back of his mind, a plan was slowly unfolding. It was dangerous, he knew; and it might mean the end of both of them. But he had to try. He couldn't continue to live this way.

"Just remember, I could make things very unpleasant for you. Do you hear me?"

Hans heard, but once again he chose not to respond. This notion of a comeback to the circus could only spell disaster. It had killed their parents. It would kill them, too. He had to stop him.

"Oh, no, you won't, you transparent little imbecile. I know what you're thinking. You hide nothing from me. When will you learn that?"

Hans held his hands over his ears, but it did no good. He began to tremble, then whimper, his face turning a ghastly white when he saw the rawhide lace in the other's hands.

"Naughty, naughty boy. Now you will have to be punished."

Hans shook convulsively. "No, please," he begged. "Not again. Please."

"Naughty boy. Now take down your pants. Drop them!" The command was undeniable.

Hans did as he was told.

He felt the rawhide coil about his testicles and he shrieked from the pain. The leather thong pulled tighter and tighter until he feared his testicles would explode.

Then darkness closed in and brought him merciful relief.

When he regained consciousness, the house was again in silence. He prayed that at last he was alone.

Minutes passed; then once again, a voice pierced the darkness.

"Tomorrow you will order more provisions. Ten pounds of fresh beef liver. This will make my cats perform. They need iron for their blood. So do you, dear Hans. You are pale and sickly looking. Someday I shall find a very special beast and I shall feed its liver to you!"

Maniacal laughter echoed through the empty halls.

Four

The aisles of Rossler's Meat & Grocery Market were empty of customers. At three o'clock on a hot Monday afternoon, the street outside was deserted as well.

Rudy Rossler, the store proprietor, stared through the front window. A loud crash spun him around.

Bobby Slater, the summer kid, had just knocked over a pyramid of Campbell's Soup cans. This was his second mishap of the day. Earlier, he'd knocked a carton of jars of tomato juice off the hand truck. Thick red liquid and broken glass had covered the entire area between the front door and the cash register.

Rudy sighed and shook his head. Maybe it was a good thing they were having a slow day. With Bobby Slater as the hired boy, it was like having no help at all. The Slater kid could be irritating as hell, but, also, he made Rudy laugh, and few people could claim that accomplishment.

His phone was ringing in the office at the back

of the store. Rudy threaded his way through the rolling cans to answer it.

"Rossler's Market, Rudy speaking," he announced with just a hint of the Germanic accent he'd spent forty years trying to lose. "So! Herr Von Ziegler. What will it be today?" Rudy listened, sitting ramrod straight in his chair, then pulled an order pad from the top drawer of his rolltop desk. He nodded repeatedly as he scribbled on the pad, then paused a moment and glanced over at the Slater boy. "All right, Herr Von Ziegler. This afternoon, for sure."

Rossler put down the phone and pursed his lips. This could be a problem.

Leaving the store to drive out to the Von Ziegler estate meant closing up for an hour or so. To remain open and allow young Bobby Slater to take over would be a gamble. The alternative was to send the boy on his bicycle to make the delivery himself. Von Ziegler was tricky business, but Rossler opted for the latter.

He cleared his throat. "Bobby!" he called, interrupting the boy just as he was to place the final can atop a bigger and better pyramid of Campbell's Tomato Soups.

The boy looked over at him, hoping his eager smile might help erase Rossler's memory of the day's misadventures.

"I've got an order for the Von Ziegler place. Do you know how to get there?"

"Sure, Mr. Rossler. I can find it." This wasn't the moment to give his employer any additional doubt as to how suited he was for the job. He'd hung on all summer and hoped to work weekends once the new school year started. This was no time to blow it.

Rossler placed a cardboard box on top of the counter and began to consult the order pad in his hand.

"I'd go there myself, but Von Ziegler is in a hurry. So! You do the job for me like a good boy."

"No problem, Mr. Rossler, honest." Bobby flashed him one of those funny grins that had saved him from getting fired at least six times during the summer. He was already thinking about something else. Everyone in town had a story about the mysterious Hans Von Ziegler. This was his big chance. Now he'd have one of his own.

When Rossler returned from the walk-in refrigerator at the back of the store, Bobby had a curious look on his face. Instinct told Rossler he was up to something.

"Oh, no, you don't, Mr. Smart Guy," Rossler warned. "I see what you're thinking and the answer is 'no'!"

Bobby opened his eyes as wide as he could and tried to put on the face he used when the parish priest caught him sipping sacramental wine in the vestry after morning mass. "I'm not thinking anything, Mr. Rossler," he replied with as much innocence as he could manage to muster.

"That's right, most of the while," Rossler harrumphed. "But this time forget it. Everybody tries to get into that place sometime or other. But let me tell you something. Von Ziegler is a good customer. He doesn't want people on his property, okay? I re-

36

spect that." Rossler was packing the cardboard box, but he went on. "You put this box on your bicycle and deliver it like you're told. You can forget about snooping around. Is that clear?"

It was. And Bobby was disappointed. His appetite for adventure had been whetted and he hated to give it up. But from the look on Rossler's face, he knew the case was closed.

Bobby was out of breath when he reached the top of the hill along the old river road. He was also drenched with sweat and felt the beads of perspiration trickling down his back. The light summer shirt he wore stuck to his skin.

Pumping up a hill like that was nearly impossible with a basket loaded with heavy groceries. He was almost ready to get off the bike and push. But that meant he was giving up, and giving up was something he refused to do. Suddenly, he found himself thinking about Hans Von Ziegler.

He still had a mile or so to go. The rest would be easy. Bobby pushed off, keeping a firm grip on the handlebars that still threatened to knock him off balance, even with the gentle downhill slope of the road.

When he reached the massive wrought-iron gate guarding the Von Ziegler property, he noticed it was caked with rust and badly in need of repair.

Bobby coasted up next to the carved stone bench that stood to one side of the gate. He climbed off his bike and gave the kickstand a shove with his foot. The bike nearly toppled over as he wrestled the large cardboard box from the basket on his handlebars.

Rossler's orders rang in his ears.

Dutifully, he placed the carton beneath the seat of the carved stone bench. Then, as instructed, he went to the mailbox by the side of the road. Just as Rossler had told him, an envelope stuffed with bills was propped up inside.

He removed it, counted the bills, replaced them with proper change, then returned the envelope to its original position and closed the box.

Bobby's curiosity was starting to assert itself. He remembered Rossler's instructions, but when would he be sent this way again? What harm could it possibly do, if he had one little peek? Von Ziegler rarely left his property and everyone who ever saw him had a different version of what he looked like. Bobby wanted one of his own.

There was a little copse of bushes on the other side of the road where he could hide his bike and sit and wait for Von Ziegler to pick up the groceries. If he'd been in such a big hurry to have them delivered, he ought to be along soon.

Without another thought, he wheeled the bike across the road. From where he was, he had a pretty clear view of the stone bench and the cardboard box beneath it. Now, all he had to do was wait.

His heart began to thump in his chest. What was the big deal? he asked himself. He was about to watch a weird guy pick up a bunch of groceries. What was so scary about that? Still, his heart continued to pound. It was almost like the wonder and fear he felt the day he and his friends found a chink in the wall at school and watched the girls getting undressed for gym class.

Only the faintest whisper of a breeze moved the tips of the pine trees that surrounded him. At last, he heard the sound of an engine. It seemed to come from the driveway behind the wrought-iron gate.

Presently, a battered 1958 blue Ford pickup came into view. Its front fenders were dented and one headlight had been knocked out. Brakes whined as it came to a halt. The motor continued to idle as a gaunt middle-aged man with a thatch of wheat-colored hair stepped down from the cab. He wore a pair of baggy workpants and an open, long-sleeved shirt over an undershirt that was torn and stained.

The family had once been very rich, or so people in the town seemed to think, nothing Bobby saw would have proven it.

A thick chain with a large metal lock held the rusting gate in place. Bobby watched as the man released the lock, gave the chain a pull, and pushed the rusty gate open. It made an eerie creaking sound as it moved. Then the man got back in the truck and rolled it closer to the road.

Now Bobby could hardly see anything. The pickup was blocking his view. He stood up slightly, straining for a better look, then ducked back, hoping he hadn't been spotted. He was about to try it again when he heard a voice scream.

"Moronic imbecile! Can't you do anything right? There's someone watching us!"

Pale with fear, Bobby crouched even lower, wondering where to go if he had to make a run for it.

"Go get him, you half-wit!" the voice ordered with terrifying determination.

Between the branches of the bushes surrounding him, Bobby could see the man with the wheat-colored hair emerge from behind the truck. He appeared to be staring about in confusion, as though not sure what he should do next. He stepped into the road, wild-eyed, and Bobby thought it looked like he had saliva foaming at the corner of his mouth. The man walked stiff-legged, as though he was in some kind of trance.

Had someone actually spotted him or was it just a good guess? Bobby decided not to wait around to find out.

A ditch ran along the side of the road, and if somehow he could make his way there without being seen, he could travel along the ditch on his hands and knees until he was far enough away to make a run for it. With luck, he could hitch a ride if a car came by and get himself as far from this place as he possibly could.

Crouching as low as he could get, he worked himself slowly toward the drainage ditch. He didn't dare raise his head to see where Von Ziegler might be now. For the moment, at least, no one was screaming any orders.

Time seemed to have stopped as Bobby waited, lying in the ditch on his stomach, hoping to hear the sound of the pickup truck heading away from the gate, back up the drive toward the stone mansion he hoped he'd never see up at the top of the hill.

A heavy rain the night before left the bottom of the ditch wet and soggy. It had a rich musky smell. As he lay there, Bobby felt it soaking through the front of his shirt and pants. He lay as still and as flat as he could, wondering what could be so bad about having a quick look at a strange guy he'd heard about all his life. He prayed the two men would give up and go away. It sure wasn't worth hunting down a kid like he was some kind of wild animal.

The blood pounding in his ears had turned into a deafening roar. It took some time for him to realize what he heard was another engine somewhere in the distance. The closer it got, the more desperate he felt. This was his only chance, but did he dare take the risk? If he stood up and ran into the road, there was no turning back.

He waited, pressed against the muddy ground until he could feel it begin to tremble. What if it was one of those heavy trailer trucks steaming along so fast it couldn't stop? Then it would be too late. This was it. He decided to make a dash for it.

His head and shoulders appeared over the edge of the ditch as he scrambled up its steep incline. Bobby plunged forward into the road, frantically flailing his arms.

A motorcycle was speeding toward him. "Stop! Please stop!" he shrieked at the top of his lungs, fully aware the driver couldn't possibly hear him above the roar of its powerful engine. "Please, please!" he continued to beg, now unable to hear the sound of his own voice either.

The big bike roared closer and closer.

Bobby's heart sank as it zoomed past. He didn't dare cast a glance down the road on the other side. He could see the pickup truck out of the corner of his eye. He didn't have to move his head.

Rooted to the spot, he hunched his shoulders and awaited the inevitable.

It took a few moments to realize he was listening to a different kind of sound. The bike had screeched to a halt a few feet away. Bobby whirled around and ran. He was out of breath and unable to speak.

"Hop on," the rider said, patting a stretch of unoccupied leather that covered the bike's large, roomy seat.

Bobby did as he was told, clutching the driver around the waist as the bike lurched forward. They sped down the road and soon he realized it was long blonde hair that was slapping him about the face. At the same moment, he had the undeniable impression what were resting on his chubby forearms were two ample, but very firm, breasts.

He didn't dare loosen his grasp, but what if she thought he was just a fresh kid, stopped the bike, and left him there? What would he do then, with two maniacs on the loose back there on the road, trying to find him?

"Thought I was a guy, didn't you?" she yelled back over her shoulder. They rode on for a bit, then she yelled again. "Where are you going?"

"Rhinelander!"

"Whereabouts?"

"Main Street! Rossler's Market!"

She punched the air with her fist like that was

42

just where she was hoping he wanted to go. Boy, thought Bobby, this is some chick. Miles down the road, when they slowed for a traffic signal, he relaxed his grip for the first time.

"My bike!" he suddenly screamed.

She slowed the cycle even more, pulled to the side of the road, and turned to face him. She was heart-stoppingly pretty, he thought, with two of the biggest dimples he'd ever seen, except on television.

The smile had taken its time, but when it got there, it was a killer. "What bike?" she asked finally.

"I left it back there," he apologized, jerking his thumb over his shoulder. "I hid it in the bushes."

"You're really a trip, you know that?"

He felt stupid and suddenly overwhelmingly shy. For the first time, he noticed his rescuer was wearing some kind of circus costume. He suddenly panicked. What if she had something to do with the Von Zieglers? Would she bring him back for the punishment he deserved for violating their rules of privacy? If that was the idea, he'd better talk fast.

"I just wanted to get a look at that guy Von Ziegler, so I hid in the bushes after I delivered his groceries?"

"So?"

"There was another guy, too. But I couldn't get a look at him. They nearly caught me."

"What if they did?"

Bobby didn't have an answer, but thinking about it made his stomach turn. He waited for her to speak.

"Who is this guy, anyway?"

43

He nearly swooned with relief. So she wasn't part of the Von Ziegler conspiracy, after all.

"His family had a circus, or something like that," he explained, giving her costume another glance. "I hear they're all dead and he lives up there by himself."

Without a word, she jumped on the starter and turned the bike around, then revved the engine and off they went. The ride was slow at first. The engine coughed, sputtered, and twice it stalled before she got it going again.

"I hope you remember where you left it," she called back to him once they were under way. This unexpected detour would make her late for work, she told him, but she really didn't mind. She tended bar over in Ruttenburg at the Stony Creek Rathskeller. Her aunt owned the place, so it wasn't likely she'd get fired.

By the time they reached the bend in the road near the big iron gate, Bobby's heart was pounding again. What would they do if the pickup truck was still parked by the side of the road? He closed his eyes as the heavy bike leaned into the turn.

When the bike began to slow, he opened his eyes and whooped aloud.

"They're gone!" he shouted.

She stopped the bike; he jumped off and scrambled through the bushes. "It's here," he yelled. "I've got it!"

As he shoved his bicycle through the underbrush, down the ravine to the drainage ditch and up the other side, she watched patiently. He mounted up and rode up next to her, smiling that same kind of lopsided grin that Rossler found so touching.

"You never told me your name," he said shyly.

"Judy," she replied, and the dimples rippled again.

"I'm Bob," he announced, suddenly feeling very grown up. "Thanks. You saved my life."

He knew she watched him for a while as he peddled off down the road.

Five

"Hey, Harry! Where's the lion tamer?"

"Late," he snorted. "What else is new?"

"Well, get the lead out, for crissake. We're dying of thirst over here!"

The bar at the Stony Creek Rathskeller was filling up. It always did when most of the working folk in town called it quits for the day. On hot afternoons like the one they just had, business was always brisk. A couple of hours of air-conditioned comfort while they tossed back a couple of cold ones, and caught up on the latest gossip was the perfect intermission between long acts of predictable routine that created the lackluster drama of most of their lives.

News of any kind traveled fast in Ruttenburg.

By midafternoon, almost anyone with a nodding acquaintance of Kathy Kraus had heard that she never returned from her weekend camping trip. The Ruttenburg police registered only mild concern when they got the call from her mother.

Officer Jim Sweeney was on duty when the call came in. It was his personal opinion that the foursome had probably hightailed it up to Canada or down to New York City for a little excitement, the kind that setting up tents and shitting in the woods for the weekend didn't quite afford.

Trudy Kraus wasn't buying. If they'd changed their plans, Kathy would have called to tell her, she was sure of it.

For his part, Jim Sweeney was not. The area had its share of missing persons, specifically young women in their late teens or early twenties, but there hadn't been many. Furthermore, there was never any reason to suspect foul play. As far as Jim was concerned, they all got out in the nick of time. A stroll through the Ruttenburg Supermarket on a Saturday afternoon was the perfect showcase for pretty young things who had peaked on the day they got married.

A good many of the town's young mothers navigating overstuffed shopping carts through the aisles of the store tipped their bathroom scales at close to two hundred pounds. Most of them had cranky toddlers tucked into the carts along with their groceries while they patrolled the store seeking out bargains. It wasn't anyone's idea of glamour, and few of them dared to dream for more.

Officer Sweeney remembered Kathy Kraus only too well. He'd taken her to the senior prom when they were in high school. It was the first time he'd ever had sex, although he'd been bragging about it since he was fourteen. They stayed out until way past dawn. Kathy's mother phoned all over town looking for Kathy that night, too.

Trudy Kraus was a born worrier.

Despite his feelings in that regard, Jim Sweeney promised to check the local hospitals. If an accident occurred over the weekend involving anyone of Kathy's description, he'd let her know right away. He'd also get on the computer to check police reports in the local area. If that yielded nothing, he'd notify the state police.

That should keep her quiet for a while, he thought. Meanwhile, he told her, she should try to relax. She'd probably hear from Kathy long before the day was out.

Trudy still wasn't buying. But just in case, she planned to stick close to her phone.

Early afternoons at the Rathskeller were never busy anyway, so when Trudy called to say something unexpected had come up, Ellen Wallace, who owned the place, told her not to rush. Trudy was about to hang up when, without any warning, she burst into tears.

Kathy had gone camping for the weekend, she sobbed. She was with friends and one of them was a guy she was more than a little interested in. Kathy was expected home Sunday night, but she never came back.

"Maybe she eloped," Ellen offered, trying to find some ray of hope to cheer her most reliable waitress, who suddenly sounded inconsolable.

"I've already called the police," Trudy replied, not giving her a chance to continue.

"You didn't!" Ellen cried. Times had changed. They weren't living in the Fifties, like she had growing up, when young people hardly ever stayed out together overnight. But even then, most mothers would have thought twice before calling in the police.

Poor Kathy, she thought. She was a sweet person but the type who could easily let people take advantage of her. If she'd taken off for a few days with some young man, maybe it was a good thing.

"Cheer up, Trudy," Ellen continued. "I'm sure you'll hear from her. If you don't feel like coming in, it's no big deal. You probably need some time for yourself."

When Ellen's divorce from Charles Hunt was final, the Stony Creek Rathskeller became hers. She wanted nothing else, just the place she'd worked so hard to build. Once it was over, she often remarked to friends that her marriage was one of the early casualties of the Sexual Revolution. And that revolution began for her when her husband, Charles Hunt, revealed he was gay, a fact he denied even to himself for most of the years of his life. Then when the Sixties came along, Charles flew out of the closet like a moth from behind locked doors, waiting for the moment for his flight to freedom.

At first she didn't understand. Nothing in life had prepared her for a husband who preferred to share his bed and exuberant sexual energies with much-younger men.

The bar at the Rathskeller rarely produced like-minded prospects. Charles had often found it necessary to travel miles from Ruttenburg for the kind of physical excitement that really satisfied him.

In the beginning, he came home very late. Then,

as time went on, he rarely came home at all. Once he met Nick, that was that.

Meanwhile, she continued to order the food, confer with salesmen who stopped by to restock the bar, and hire and fire waitresses and bartenders. Most of the time she ran the place by herself.

Her divorce decree was folded neatly and stored in the office safe the day Harry Wallace pulled into the Rathskeller parking lot. He'd been to the races that week up at Saratoga and was cleaned out. A few crumpled bills were all that was left in his pocket after seven days of high living and heavy betting. If the Rathskeller could use the services of an ex-Army cook, Harry told her, he was for hire.

She could scarcely believe her ears. Or her eyes.

Harry Wallace was handsome in a ruined, brutally masculine kind of way. His hair and eyes were almost the same chestnut brown, and there were deeply etched lines at the corners of his eyes and mouth that intensified when he smiled. His nose had been flattened at its bridge during a brief career as an amateur boxer, yet the effect was oddly appealing.

It was his mouth that knocked her socks off. It was small but the lips were full and sensuous. When they weren't engaged in speaking, his lips appeared to be constantly puckered, as if demanding to be kissed.

Ellen would have hired him, even if he couldn't cook.

Harry popped the caps from two ice-cold bottles of Budweiser and slid them along the bar to the town's only plumber and his assistant.

"When the lion tamer hangs out at the other end of the bar, there's a dynamite view. Your ass doesn't make it," the plumber laughed.

This was the kind of conversation that gave Harry a giant pain. He preferred the company of a blistering stove back in the kitchen to a couple of jerks who acted like they were trying out for jobs as standup comics. At six o'clock in the afternoon, the place was always full of them. The later it got, the funnier they thought they were.

Furthermore, it started to look like Ellen would wear a hole in the carpet, rushing back and forth from the kitchen to the dining room and back to the bar. As he watched her place a tray of dirty glasses in front of him, he couldn't deny the surge of admiration he felt for her.

Ellen was tough. Not tough to look at, but deep inside she had a strength Harry knew he would never equal.

She'd gained a little weight since they got married, but he thought it made her sexier. As far as Harry was concerned, Ellen was too skinny when they first met. The unhappy relationship leading to divorce from her first husband had taken its toll.

Now, in her midforties, she was still almost prom-queen pretty with the same great dimples that ran in the family. Her light brown, shoulder-length hair started to show streaks of gray which regular frostings at the beauty parlor had somehow turned into a plus. When she was on duty at the Rathskeller, Ellen kept it pinned in a sleek French twist.

Harry thought Ellen was a real class act, but it wasn't in his nature for him to say so.

"If that niece of yours ever shows up, maybe I can get out from here and give you a hand," he muttered as he plunged the dirty glassware into hot, sudsy water.

"Don't bug me about her tonight, okay?" Ellen snapped. A strand of hair had come loose at the back of her neck and she wore an expression that told him the subject of Judy McAuliffe was completely off limits.

God, he thought, everyone's walking on eggs today. Kathy Kraus gets lucky and these women are all acting like someone fucked the Virgin Mary. Kathy was a nice kid, but she'd had more pricks stuck in her than a porcupine, his included. It wasn't something he was especially proud of. In fact, if Ellen ever found out, he'd be in the shithouse for longer than he cared to imagine.

It was right around New Year's, that night when Trudy called in sick and Kathy took over her shift. She was on vacation from college at the time and had some old heap of a car that refused to start when it was time to go home. Harry'd been having a couple of holiday drinks with some of the Rathskeller regulars when Kathy came back and asked him for help. He felt sorry for the kid, but there was something about her that attracted him, too. She was like an overstuffed sofa he wanted to land on, just to see if it was as soft and comfy as it looked.

What really clinched the deal was that while they were sitting in that old car of hers she confessed she had trouble having an orgasm.

Christ, Harry thought later, I'm like an old Dalmatian when he hears a fire truck. Look at me, sitting right up there in the front seat with my tongue hanging out, rarin' to go!

At the time, he thought he'd done the girl a favor. He prayed that was the end of it and she'd forget it ever happened. But once Ellen's niece arrived on the scene, the two of them would get together every once in a while and later he'd catch Judy giving him some pretty funny looks. The odds weren't with him and he knew it.

It was almost a year to the day since Judy McAuliffe rolled into the parking lot of the Stony Creek Rathskeller, astride her 1973 Harley-Davidson. She was eighteen years old at the time and her mother had died a few months earlier. Her mother was Ellen's only sister. Judy, the only daughter and only child, was broke. What else could Ellen do but take the kid in and give her a job?

Besides, Harry hated tending bar. She was doing him a favor.

Judy insisted that within a few months she'd have saved enough money to head south before winter really set in. Then, she planned to hook up with a big, international circus while it took its winter layover in Florida.

Harry knew Ellen thought the scheme was utterly hairbrained, but why deflate the dreams of a determined young thing, poised so breathlessly on the threshold of life? Besides, by the time winter rolled around, Judy probably wouldn't have enough saved to get her farther south than Philadelphia. But, for the time being, it was best to say nothing. Just wait. Time and the facts would speak for themselves.

* * *

"Yahoo!" came a shout from the end of the bar. Someone else whistled, and all heads snapped around as Judy strode through the front door.

Yanking at the chin strap, she pulled off the motorcycle helmet, producing a cascade of wind-tossed blonde hair. She wiggled past Harry to her customary position behind the bar.

A damp, soggy towel was stuffed in his belt. Harry gave it a tug and threw it down beside her.

"Where the hell were you?" he demanded. "Signing autographs?"

"On an errand of mercy, if you must know," she replied, favoring him with the kind of smile that never failed to make him mad.

He shoved his way past the swinging doors next to the bar, marched through the kitchen and out the back door. The sun had set, leaving behind a faint wash of violet in a cloudless sky. Not a leaf rustled. Harry lit a cigarette. Quite frankly, the more he thought about Kathy Kraus the more worried he became.

What the hell was wrong with Trudy, calling the cops like that? Give the kid a little space, for crissake. But what if she didn't take off with her camping pals? He began to run through the possibilities. If she'd been in an accident, they'd know soon enough. If she'd gotten herself in some kind of trouble, he sure hoped no one would come snooping around the Rathskeller asking a lot of questions.

That kind of thing had a way of turning up information no one was looking for, and Harry's stomach turned over just thinking about it. He and Ellen had a pretty good life together. He could keep it that way, if everyone would mind their own business for a while.

The rows of bottles that lined the bar in front of the mirror made it hard for Judy to get a good look at herself. Running her fingers through her hair, she pulled the long strands at the crown straight in the air, then let them fall. It was all part of the tousled, wild-animal look she was cultivating.

Her tips had doubled since she started wearing the little red jacket with the gold braid, skintight white jeans, and boots that came up to her knees.

"Get over here, you wild thing," the plumber called to her. "One of these days someone's going to have to put you in a cage."

Judy stole another glance in the mirror, then moved along the bar toward the plumber and his assistant. A crumpled five-dollar bill lay on the bar in front of them. Was this an enticement for better service or would he shove it back in his pocket like he did the last time, leaving only a buck as thanks for time spent listening to boring tales of plugged-up sinks and flooding toilets?

She didn't have a lot of options, not if she wanted to head for Florida before the weather got too nasty for travel by motorcycle.

"Get those cute buns over here," the plumber ordered. "We got a couple of jokes that'll knock your socks off."

Judy sloshed house whiskey into a couple of shot glasses, then leaned over and reached into the refrigerator behind the bar. She could feel his eyes riveted to her backside. Maybe the jeans were too tight, she thought, but the circus outfit had done the trick. She'd put away more money the week she started wearing it than she had the entire month before.

It sure didn't take much to get these clowns excited.

Her aunt was pushing a tray of empties in her direction. "I wish you'd call us, if you're going to be late for work," she chided.

"It's broad daylight, for crying out loud! What are you so worried about?"

Ellen bit the inside of her lip. "Sorry, honey. I don't mean to be a nuisance. Trudy's daughter is still missing. It's got me a bit on edge."

"Everybody thinks she and that guy just took off. Can't say I blame her."

The look on Ellen's face registered genuine pain. "You wouldn't do a thing like that!"

"Auntie, this town is nowhere. Anybody around here with any get-up-and-go got up and went a long time ago. Present company excluded, of course."

The pay phone next to the rest rooms began to ring and Ellen hurried to answer it. The bar was getting noisy and someone put a dollar's worth of quarters in the jukebox. She could barely make out Jim Sweeney's voice at the other end. All she knew was that he wanted to stop by the Rathskeller and ask a few questions.

Six

The following day there was still no word from Kathy Kraus. The silence of the telephone had sent Trudy back to the comforting mindless din of the Rathskeller. Jim Sweeney's preliminary investigations yielded nothing.

Judy was behind the bar when Bud Mosher, owner of the gas station over on Route 32, ambled in and perched his lanky frame astride one of the stools.

"What's it going to be tonight?" she asked, refusing to make eye contact with him.

"Let's see, now," he began, as though contemplating the table of contents to her bartenders' manual. "I think I'll try one of those beautiful Tequila Sunsets."

She waited for him to change his mind. No one drank stuff like that at the Rathskeller. This was a beer-and-backup kind of place. Once in a while, some of the dinner customers would order wine by the glass, but that was pretty much it.

If Bud was testing her, she'd call his bluff. She knew the manual cold, even though she never needed it. *"Si, señor!"* she mumbled at the row of bottles behind the bar while searching for the proper ingredients.

Into a stainless-steel cocktail shaker went the tequila, grenadine, orange juice, and a shovelful of chopped ice. She gave it all a ferocious shake and poured the results into a frosty stemmed glass. For the first time in a long while, Judy felt self-conscious. She felt like Bud was silently evaluating everything she did and had already put a grade on it.

He tasted the drink, then licked his lips.

"Not bad," he observed quietly. "Not like I've had 'em before, but not bad."

Who was he kidding, she thought, and where the hell did he ever drink Tequila Sunsets before? Not at the Rathskeller, that was for sure, and the Rathskeller was the only game in town.

Behind the bar the temperature was a good ten degrees hotter than it was on the other side. The stiff gold-braided jacket was making her sweat. She unfastened it halfway down the front and turned away. A sidelong glance revealed a lot of loose change lying around. No big tippers anywhere in sight. She moved in the direction of three new arrivals and smiled her dimpliest, most-revenue-producing smile.

"Looks like this end of the bar could use some attention," she purred.

"That's not all we could use," one of them winked.

She looked around, wondering if Bud had any reaction to the three newcomers, and saw that he'd disappeared.

"When d'you blow this joint?" one of them asked.

"I don't," she smiled. "I live upstairs."

Bud had taken his Tequila Sunset and moved into the dining room, where Ellen led him to a small table next to the window overlooking the parking lot. Bud liked this table. It provided a special view of who was coming and going, at what time, and with whom. He wasn't a gossip, but he was a businessman. He liked having his facts straight when people came around asking for a deal on a new set of tires or any myriad of items that might be negotiable.

Outside, a swirling red light announced the arrival of Ruttenburg police, minutes before the blue-and-yellow vehicle pulled into view.

Trudy looked up, like a deer in the woods sensing imminent danger.

Both front doors flew open. Out sprang Officer Lawrence Sweeney and his younger brother, Jim. They were only a year apart in age, what some people called "Irish twins." While they were both in high school, the pair were notorious for the number of brawls they could instigate on any given weekend. A couple of Irish teenagers with a fifth of Imperial Whiskey could wreck a party, a dance, or just a bunch of guys hanging out on the corner.

When Lawrence Sweeney entered the police academy, nobody believed he'd last. When Jim entered a year later, they guffawed. When they graduated, the old gang dubbed them "Law and Order." The new names stuck.

Sipping his Tequila Sunset, Bud watched as the two made their way around the patrol car to the front entrance of the Rathskeller.

"We'd like a word with Mrs. Kraus," Law informed Ellen quietly, when he and Jim came through the door. He stroked a bushlike mustache and his beady blue eyes roamed the room.

Ellen indicated a table at the back of the restaurant where Trudy stood, her face now gone ashen.

"Law and Order" wove their way through the tables, found an empty one in a corner, and beckoned for Trudy to join them.

Jim Sweeney had a leather-covered notepad, which he placed on the table in front of him. They'd already decided he'd take the notes while Law asked the questions.

Once they'd gotten their badges, Lawrence Sweeney turned very serious. Jim was still the laid-back, gregarious guy he'd always been. He loved a good joke. With his straight nose, strong determined jawline, and deep blue eyes, he was almost movie-star handsome. When it came time to playing "Good Cop, Bad Cop," it was perfectly clear who was who.

Trudy sat down, looking anxiously first at Lawrence, then at Jim. How could life have played her such a dirty trick? she wondered. A couple of years back, if there were trouble in town, one of these Sweeneys was sure to be smack in the middle of it. Maybe both. Kathy had never been in trouble but since she disappeared, people kept acting like she did something wrong.

"Have you heard something?" she asked hesitantly, almost afraid to hear the answer.

"Nothing yet. We have to ask you a few more questions, if you can spare us the time."

She was beside herself with fear and these two were asking if she could spare the time.

"Does the name Christine Vincent mean anything to you?"

Trudy shrugged and shook her head.

"Peggy Moynihan?"

No response.

"How about Charlene Connors?"

Again Trudy shook her head. "Who are they?"

"Three young, female Missing Persons. Just a hunch."

"What kind of hunch?"

"One's from over in Bennewater, one's from Creek Locks, and this Conner kid is from Rhinelander, actually."

"I don't get your point."

The brothers exchanged a look and Trudy wanted to slap their faces. They were driving at something and she didn't like it.

"Let me put it this way, Miz Kraus," Law began. "These are three runaways from the area who disappeared within the last year. No contact's been made with their families yet but they're still hoping."

Trudy stared from Law to Jim and back again. "And you think that's what happened to my Kathy." Her voice lowered. "Now I'll tell you something. It's what I've said all along. Somethin' happened. I don't know what, exactly, but that's what you guys get paid to find out."

"It's not easy telling parents stuff they don't want to hear," Law continued. "The bad part is that when these runaways get where they're going, they haven't got anything to live on. Pimps hang around the bus stations just waiting for fresh meat."

"Stop it!" Trudy yelled, then looked around, hoping none of the customers had heard. "Kathy's not that kind of girl and you know it." Her gaze then fell on Jim Sweeney, who was rolling his ballpoint pen between the palms of his hands.

He kept on rolling the pen when he answered. "These are the only leads we got, Miz Kraus. Maybe Kathy knew one of them. Maybe they all talked about getting out of town for good. I don't know. And you don't know, either."

"Then I'll tell you what I do know. She's someplace, that's for darn sure. If you boys are half as smart as you'd like for people to think you are, then I say you better find her!"

With a move of the head that was scarcely visible, Law Sweeney told his brother the interview was over. He pushed back his chair. Jim followed. The two rose as one and moved toward the door. "We'll be in touch, Miz Kraus," Law stated flatly.

"See that you do," she called after them, then pushed her way through the tables and headed for the ladies' rest room.

Sensing that Trudy was very upset, Ellen followed after her. It was a tiny little room with hardly enough space for a single occupant. Trudy was leaning over the basin, throwing cold water on her face, when she looked up and saw Ellen behind her in the mirror.

"Any news?" Ellen asked softly.

"Those two couldn't find their own shit in a toilet bowl!" she exploded. "Put a uniform on 'em and they think they know everything."

"They haven't had much time," Ellen replied, hoping to help Trudy keep things in some kind of perspective.

"They had enough time to find out all the run-aways from this neck of the woods. I know a closed mind when I see one. Those two think they've got the whole thing figured out."

Ellen hesitated. In her heart, she had to agree with what the Sweeneys were suggesting. They'd just have to wait and see. "Are you going to be okay?" she asked, quite prepared to let Trudy go home, if she wanted to.

"I'm not gonna be okay until my Kathy is home where she belongs," she stated resolutely. "Let me go back to my tables. It'll help me get my mind off things, at least for a little while." Trudy sniffed, patted her hair, then turned and marched through the door.

Ellen leaned against the sink and sighed.

Perspiration dripped from Harry's brow. With a long-tined fork, he speared one steak, then another, and flipped them over. Their sizzle made such a racket he never heard the Sweeney brothers come through the kitchen door. He whirled about as Law Sweeney addressed him.

"Can you talk and cook at the same time or should we go outside?"

Jim Sweeney threw him one of his lopsided, easy grins; and for a split second, Harry relaxed. But then, looking back at Law, he felt a twinge of panic stab at his gut. Did these guys suspect something?

"Frankly, Harry" — Law Sweeney began moving to a spot where the heat wasn't quite so intense — "we're between a rock and a hard place. We have our ideas about Kathy Kraus; her mother's got hers. What we have to do now is spend a week or so asking questions that'll end up with us being right and her being wrong."

Harry glanced back and forth between the two, wondering what, exactly, those ideas were.

"She worked here, right?" Jim asked.

"Filled in for her mother. It wasn't a regular job," Harry answered. "Back here, I don't see much of the waitresses. They come in, place their orders, go back for more, pick up their orders, bring 'em out to the customers. Like that." As if to demonstrate, he lifted the steaks, so they both dangled from the end of the fork, then dropped them, each on a separate plate. He gave the french fry basket a shake. It popped and splattered until Harry lifted it from the hot fat.

The combination of smells wafting through the kitchen made Jim's mouth water. He thought about stealing a couple of french fries, but he knew Law wouldn't like it.

"Think she was having trouble at home?" he heard his brother ask as he felt a new gurgle begin.

In the back of his mind, Harry tried to figure his position. He could be the guy who rarely came out of the kitchen, except when they were shorthanded and the customers were more interested in what they were drinking than what they had to eat. Basically, this was true. But when the kitchen closed, he often sat at the bar, having a couple of "pops" before they closed up for the night.

He'd had a pretty active love life before he got cleaned out that summer at Saratoga. One of his nightmares involved some chick from the old days arriving at the Rathskeller, unannounced, declaring him to be the father of some prepubescent kid. In reality, this dream might have applied to a dozen or so. Harry had reason to believe he might have at least a couple of unacknowledged offspring, all living within the state lines.

In fact, he made it a rule to take a really good look through the small square of glass in the swinging doors next to the bar when the kitchen closed at the end of the night.

"You must have had some conversation with her," Law Sweeney was saying when Harry once again began to focus on the two young men standing next to the refrigerator in their short-sleeved summer police uniforms.

"Sure. But nothing I can really recall."

"Did you ever drive her home, or anything like that?"

"Just a fucking minute!" Harry protested, instantly aware that he'd overreacted. He could feel tiny pinpoints of heat prickle down his back. He almost blew it. These two kids didn't know anything. It was a legitimate question, but he'd let it throw him.

"Hey, man," Jim replied. "Don't get the wrong idea. We're just looking for leads. If you spent any time with her, she might have opened up to you." He glanced over at the fry basket again. "Excuse me, could I have one of those?"

"Sure, help yourself," Harry beamed, emptying the basket just the way Jim hoped he would.

Ellen rushed through the doors, carrying a tray. She snatched at the steak plates. "Where's the corn?" she demanded.

"Whoops," came Harry's lame attempt at self-deprecation. With a pair of tongs, he explored the depths of a large pot of steaming water. He smiled triumphantly back at Ellen as he placed first one then another ear of corn between the steak and french fries on each of the plates.

Without a word, Ellen hoisted the tray and was gone.

The interlude had relaxed him. "So, where were we?" Harry asked, squarely facing the Sweeney brothers once again.

"A lot of young people have trouble communicating with their parents. Sometimes they'll open up to someone else, particularly if it's someone they respect," Law Sweeney went on.

The kind of advice Harry gave Kathy Kraus wasn't something he planned to discuss with the Sweeney brothers.

"Now that I think about it, I may have given Kathy a ride home once. But that was at least a year ago." His conscience was clear. He told them of the incident of his own free will. No one had to pry it from him.

"Did she tell you anything you might remember?" Jim inquired, nonchalantly nibbling the tip of a french fry.

Yes, she did, he thought to himself. She told me you fucked her the night of the senior prom, but there were no fireworks. You tried it a couple of times again, then the two of you called it quits. She tried it again when she got to college. In fact, she tried it a lot, it was never any good. So there we were in that old Chevrolet that wouldn't start, and I told her she just hadn't met the right guy yet. She probably needed someone older and more experienced. The more I talked, the harder I got. I talked her through it like a Dutch uncle. I sounded like Masters and Johnson, for crissake, in the back seat of her old Chevrolet. God, it was freezing, but after a while it didn't seem to matter. We gave off enough heat to steam the windows. When that kid Kathy started to scream "Oh, oh, oh God, oh!" I felt like Columbus discovering America.

"What about your niece, Harry?" Law suddenly asked.

"What about her?" he demanded.

"Do you think she could help?"

"I doubt it," he replied. This was getting too close.

"You never know," Law suggested. "They were closer in age. Maybe she'd tell Judy things she wouldn't tell anyone else."

"Judy started working here after Kathy went off to college. They hardly ever saw each other."

"Couldn't hurt if we talked to her."

Harry shrugged noncommittally. "I think it's a waste of time. But go ahead if you think you have to."

Then, as if on cue, Judy sailed through the kitchen door. "Two burgers for the bar," she ordered, then looked at the Sweeneys in complete surprise. "Grabbing freebies in the kitchen?" she inquired, although she didn't really care.

"We'd like to talk to you," Jim offered.

"Busy night. Unless you're big tippers. Which I doubt, judging from the uniforms."

"How about tomorrow morning at the police station? Say, ten o'clock?"

"Why not? It doesn't get going around here until happy hour."

"See you then." Jim Sweeney smiled. He ate two more fries, saluted Harry, and followed right behind his brother as they exited through the swinging doors.

Seven

His coffee was cold when Judy came down for breakfast. Harry returned it to the pot to warm it, but the cup slid from his hands before he could get back to the chicken-salad luncheon special he was preparing.

"Shit!" he exclaimed, jumping out of the way to avoid being splashed. His favorite carving knife clattered to the floor. "Goddammit!"

Judy smiled benignly, a secret smugness coming over her to see him get so flustered over nothing. Judy was unflappable. "I'll get that," she offered, picking up a sponge from the sideboard next to the sink.

With a couple of swipes, the floor was clean and Judy returned to the sink to rinse the sponge.

Harry lit a cigarette and watched her remove a pitcher of orange juice from the restaurant-sized refrigerator. "You don't have to go," he offered, hoping he sounded more casual than he felt.

"Go where?"

"That Sweeney kid. You don't have to talk to him

if you don't feel like it. It's not like he's got a sub-poena or anything like that."

"I've never been in a police station, have you?"

This was a line of conversation Harry refused to pursue.

"What do you want to bet she's back home already?"

"Do they still hang up pictures of the Ten Most Wanted Criminals and stuff like that?"

"If you want my opinion, Trudy pushed the panic button. She's going to be very embarrassed when Kathy shows up and tells her she was gone for a few days 'cause she just had an abortion."

Judy whirled around and stared at him. "That's the trouble with this place. All anybody ever thinks about is who's getting it, who just got it, and with who! God, all of you make me sick." She gulped the glass of juice and stormed out the kitchen door.

She pulled the chin strap tight, adjusted her helmet, and headed for the corner of the parking lot where she always parked the bike.

The damn thing was gone! Her heart sank. There went all her plans. She was pacing around in a tight little circle when the crunch of gravel and the sound of a heavy motor right behind her made her jump for safety.

Bud Mosher's service-station truck pulled up alongside. Her bike was standing up in the back. Before she could say a word, Bud leaned his arm half-way out the window and smiled. "I took the liberty when I left last night."

"You took what?" she demanded, not sure if she should be mad or grateful.

"I heard you talking about the old thing and the trouble you've had with it lately, so I figured I'd look it over and give you an expert's advice."

What nerve, she thought, but decided not to express her anger until she found out what he was really up to. If it was a free overhaul, she'd keep her mouth shut. "And?"

"I've given the engine a good look. I broke it down and cleaned and oiled the parts," Bud told her. "It's okay now, but I can't guarantee for how long."

"Will it get me as far as Florida?"

"Maybe."

"Maybe what?"

"Maybe it will. Maybe it won't."

She was starting to feel vulnerable again and she didn't like it. "Bud, c'mon. Don't jerk me around."

"I'm telling it like it is. You want to get to Florida for sure, get yourself another bike."

"But I can't afford it!"

"Then don't go to Florida."

So that's what he's up to, she thought. Why was it no one could understand she didn't belong in this town? It was okay, if you never wanted any big surprises out of life. But she was too young to settle for that. A lot was going on in the world and Judy wanted to see at least some of it before she got too old to care. Everybody told her this circus idea of hers was crazy, but what was wrong with doing something a little bit crazy if she wanted to? Her mother was gone. She never knew her father. She had nobody to answer to — not yet, anyway.

One of these days, maybe she'd meet a guy who could change her mind, but so far, so good. Bud had tried his darnedest and it wasn't good enough. He was tall and sinewy without a hint of fat on his hard, long frame. Above all, he was extremely decent. Sexually, she found him extremely attractive, but she wasn't about to let him know. Otherwise, Judy stood a good chance of being like all the other young matrons winding their way through the aisles of the Ruttenburg Supermarket. That was something she had no intention of doing.

If trying to get a job in the circus sounded crazy, it sure beat some of the alternatives. No one ever did anything that was crazy in Ruttenburg. Why shouldn't she be the first?

Judy realized she was staring at Bud as if he were the enemy. He just doesn't get it, she thought. He doesn't understand.

She threw one leg over the bike, jumped on the starter, and revved the engine. She liked the way it sounded. Maybe he was wrong.

"You do nice work," she yelled, throttled up, and thundered out of the parking lot, kicking up a spray of pebbles as she sped off and down the road.

That morning when he opened the meat storage locker, there was a large package wrapped in white butcher paper he didn't remember seeing before. Careful not to spill its contents as he removed it from the shelf, Hans carried it to the counter. It was heavier than he expected and the wrapping was taped shut. With one of the knives he always kept close-by, he slit one side, then the other.

Onto the table slithered first one large blood-red

organ, then another. Two enormous livers lay on the butcher block in front of him. This was nothing he'd ordered from Rossler's market. Where had they come from?

Hans was a meticulous butcher himself. He knew precisely what had been cut up, from which animal, and when. It was all carefully documented in a notebook he kept on a shelf above the refrigerator, and just for good measure, he noted dates on the white storage paper he used to wrap the meat before placing it in the freezer.

He began to fret. The headaches had been so bad and so frequent lately, he wondered what else might have happened while he wasn't himself. Distractedly, he began to fold the liver back into the paper that had covered it when he noticed a pencil scrawl on the underside. It said, *Chew on this, you chicken-livered weakling! Your blood is weaker than dishwater!*

Hans began to tremble. The livers slid from the paper off the table and onto the floor. One was more slippery to handle than the other. They were both covered with fresh, warm blood that storage in the meat locker had not yet chilled. How long had they been there? Hans wondered. It was liver that looked just like those he'd fed to the cats the day his mother and father were mauled to death in the ring. His head began to throb again and he vomited on the floor.

The moment Judy passed through the doors of Ruttenburg's police station she noticed the unmistakable odor of industrial cleaning products in the air. The hardwood floor was heavily pitted and polished to a glossy sheen. The station's drab colors were a perfect reflection of the town it stood to protect, Judy thought. Two shades of brown, and a little tan thrown in to break things up.

Down the hall were a couple of empty cells, occupied on most occasions by weekend drunks hauled out of cars and brought in to sleep it off before they killed themselves or someone else.

Before she had a chance to ask someone where to find Jim Sweeney, she heard his voice behind her.

"Hey, thanks. I wasn't sure I'd see you this morning."

"I keep my word."

"Even better," he smiled and opened a frost-paned door, indicating she should enter.

It was a plain room with a large desk in front of a window. Hard plastic chairs with metal legs were shoved against the walls. He pulled one of them toward the desk and held it for her while she sat down.

As he rounded the desk, Jim tripped on the corner of the leg before he sat down, then he grinned. "Stuff like that wrecks the image."

She smiled back. "So?"

"This isn't an official interrogation, if that's what you're wondering. I thought it would be better if we talked here without the Rathskeller regulars staring at us."

"Shoot."

"What's your take on Kathy Kraus?"

"Personally?"

"Anything you like."

"A little too boring for my taste. But she was okay. She and her mother still lived together, but that's not so strange these days. Nobody's got any bucks."

"Was she in trouble financially?"

"She taught school. Nobody makes a fortune doing that. But I never heard her complain."

"Was she in any other kind of trouble?"

Judy gave him a long look. Didn't anybody have any imagination around here?

"Was she pregnant, is that what you're asking?"

It took Jim a moment to reply. "No. But since you brought it up, was she?"

"How would I know?"

"Trouble can mean a lot of things. So why don't we start with drugs."

"I don't think so."

"Why not?"

"I didn't spend a lot of time with her, just around the Rathskeller when she filled in for her mom. But people tell you things, even if they don't know you very well."

"Like what?"

"Hints about who they like, who they don't like, who they'd like to sleep with. That kind of stuff."

"Who was she sleeping with?"

Again Judy paused, took a long look at Officer Jim Sweeney, and stared out the window. A squirrel ran along the branch of a tree, leaped to another, then scrambled down its trunk and disappeared across the lawn out front.

"I really don't know," she answered at last.

Jim Sweeney pushed back his chair. The sound of its legs scraping the floor reminded Judy they were in a police station and, officially or not, she was here being questioned.

Her eyes roamed the room. "Is this being taped?"

75

He laughed aloud. "You've got that much to tell me?"

Once more a sense of vulnerability swept over her. She hated feeling this unsure of herself. Sweeney was a friendly kind of guy and not much older than she was. Sheer curiosity was all that brought her here this morning. Maybe she should have paid more attention to what her uncle was saying. Had she already said more than she should?

"What about your uncle?"

The question nearly made her jump from her chair. That was the moment she realized her thighs were beginning to stick to its plastic seat.

"What about him?"

"Get along, do you?"

"Okay."

"And your aunt?"

"My aunt, what?"

"Are they okay?"

"Do you want to know about their sex life, too?" She was starting to get mad. This nice pleasant guy wasn't so nice and pleasant, after all.

"He's a good-looking guy. He's been around the track a few times. I doubt he was a virgin when he landed in Ruttenburg. Some guys take their marriage vows very seriously, others don't. It's no big deal."

"And who are you fucking these days, Officer Sweeney?"

It was his turn to blink. The question caught him blindsided. It took a moment, then he laughed again. "No one. Maybe that's my problem."

Judy pulled her chair closer to his desk and stared

straight at him. "If you want to know the truth, I came here this morning because I thought it would be fun. I've never been in a police station. There are lots of places I've never been, but if I had the chance, I'd go. This was one of them." She stared him right in the eye and spoke very softly. "I promise you, I don't know anything about Kathy Kraus that's any help."

"Thanks anyway," he said, assuming she was about to leave. But she didn't.

"Now it's my turn to ask some questions," she was saying when he finally realized the interview had changed focus.

"Fair enough."

"I just heard about a family named Von Ziegler that lived over in Rhinelander."

"Right."

"What about them?"

"There's not much to tell anymore. They were a famous German circus family who came to the States during the Second World War. It's long before my time, but I hear the Von Zieglers were on Hitler's shit list for some reason. Maybe they were Jews, I don't know. Anyway they came to the States and joined up with the Ringling Brothers. They were both killed in the ring in some kind of freak accident. They owned that property over in Rhinelander where the son lives now."

"Does he live there alone?"

"As far as I know. But he's a real screwball."

"Have you ever met him?"

"Christ Almighty, no! I wouldn't go near the place."

"Why not?"

"I'm telling you, the guy's weird. He doesn't want anyone on his property and I'm very happy to oblige."

"What's his problem?"

"From what the older folks around have to say, he was still fairly young when the parents were killed. It did something to him. I think he was in the nuthouse for a while. Look, if he doesn't bother anyone, why should we bother him? That's cool, if you want my opinion."

A police radio on Sweeney's desk began to crackle.

"Ruttenburg Police, this is Ryan on the fire-department ambulance, do you read me?"

Sweeney picked up the handset and spoke into it. "Ryan, this is Sweeney. I copy. Ten Four."

The set continued to crackle, then the voice came back. "We're responding to a nine-one-one. Possible drowning over at Stony Creek, near the boat landing."

Jim leaned forward, as though the police receiver were a crystal ball and everything he needed to know was within its swirling mist. "Any description of the victim?"

"White, female. Blonde, heavyset. Early twenties. Thought it might be your Missing Person."

"Thanks, Ryan," Jim stated flatly into the microphone. "I'm on my way. Over and out."

He'd felt his throat go dry and tried to work up some saliva. He swallowed hard, then shoved his hands deep in his pockets and stared out the window, utterly unaware that he was not alone. The hands in his pockets were shaking and there was a queasy feeling at the pit of his stomach.

The relationship with Kathy Kraus had been over the summer after the senior prom, but it was special regardless of what he'd tried to tell himself later. Between her ample thighs, at last, he'd become a man. He could stop making up stories. It was hot and exciting. He probably came too fast but he learned how to hold back later. By now, he thought he was pretty good at it. Pity there was no one to practice with, then he remembered Judy. He turned and stared at her.

Judy's eyes were glistening with anticipation. "Can I come?" she asked.

"Forget it," he snapped.

"Please. I've never seen anything like this."

Suddenly, he felt very old. He was all business.

"Listen, kid. Once in a while in this life, you're going to miss out on things. Get used to it."

He grabbed for his cap, slammed it hard on the top of his head, and raced from the room.

Eight

Placing the traps had become extremely risky business. Once dug, he had to cart away the dirt that had been removed. He needed easy access for a speedy and unseen getaway, yet placing them too close to a frequently traveled path or roadway was to court disaster.

Thus far, he'd been lucky.

Yet he still hadn't landed the prized beast he so desperately sought. Without that, his plan could not go forward.

Before dawn that morning his eyes slammed open, all senses instantly alert. One of the traps had yielded prey. He stumbled about at first light, searching for his clothes. Why was it he could never find them? There were items of clothing all around, but none of them were his.

He pulled on a pair of shabby overalls and a torn shirt, hoping all the necessary equipment was still neatly placed in the rear of the truck.

It was.

The crowd hushed and pressed closer to the top of the embankment. Two paramedics had placed a collapsed gurney at the side of the road.

The first to appear were a pair of firemen with oxygen tanks strapped to their backs as they climbed over the guard rail. Then came two more, carrying a slinglike contraption created by tying up the ends of a large woolen blanket. A limp white hand protruded from one end of the blanket and a foot from the other. The firemen grunted audibly as they deposited their cargo on the gurney.

The blanket fell away. There was a dark bruise on the forehead and the face was now a bloated pale blue, her lips a deep purple. They were slightly parted in a ghoulish smirk displaying the fact that her front teeth had been broken and chipped. A mass of muddy ringlets surrounded her face, but it was her tiny feet that disturbed Judy most of all. The tops of her insteps had been rubbed raw in a last, desperate attempt to free herself from whatever it was that had pulled her to a watery grave.

Someone nearby said that an overturned canoe had been found wedged between two rocks in the rolling rapids several miles above Pebble Beach. A pink sweatshirt was found floating further downstream.

It wasn't Kathy Kraus and no one saw the tiny bullet hole under her arm.

That afternoon, while she set up for the Rathskeller's happy hour, Judy couldn't erase the image of that poor creature's bloated blue face. They were probably close to the same age, she thought. Whatever hopes that poor thing had for the life before her were ended that morning. Life was over and done with almost before it began.

What a bummer, Judy thought while she rubbed the bar with a damp sponge. I wonder if the poor girl ever had any fun. It was yet one more reason to get out of this place before another winter set in. The start of the Labor Day weekend was a couple of days off. If things went her way, the Rathskeller would be jumping. She'd run her tail off, if she had to. Maybe she could even triple her tips.

She found herself remembering what Jim Sweeney had told her about the Von Ziegler family.

What if she went over there and told him about her plans? If his parents had appeared in the Ringling Brothers circus, he must know a lot about it. He could probably give her some tips. Maybe he knew people he could introduce her to. She began to fantasize about riding up to the circus compound in Florida with a long letter of introduction in her pocket.

I have met with Judy McAuliffe and find her to be a hard-working person who is eager to learn anything and everything you care to teach her. Given the close association my family had as world-renowned animal trainers, I believe you would find her an excellent apprentice for training toward a career as a featured performer in the act . . . The imaginary letter trailed off when the phone began to ring.

Ellen hurried to answer.

"Stony Creek Rathskeller, Ellen Wallace speaking. She listened gravely, then replied, "There hasn't been

82

any news, I'm afraid. We had a bad scare earlier today, but the poor girl turned out to be someone else."

There it was again, the blue face that had moved in on Judy's memory bank. She tried to think of herself, astride her bike, gunning her way south toward a new kind of life. When Ellen came over to the bar, Judy decided there was no reason not to ask her aunt point blank.

"Do you know anything about that Von Ziegler family over in Rhinelander?"

"All I know is it's a good place to stay away from."

"Why?"

Ellen was drying glasses and placing them on the shelf behind the bar. "All I've heard are a bunch of rumors, but I'd steer pretty clear of that place if I were you."

"I bet that guy could help me."

Ellen slammed down the glass she was wiping and broke it in pieces. "Now see what you've done! It's bad enough worrying about poor Kathy Kraus, wondering if we'll ever see that girl of hers again. And here you are talking about making friends with a hermit no one ever sees for months at a time. Who knows what goes on over there!"

"Would it be so terrible if I went there and tried to find out?"

"Most likely."

"The guy may be a little strange, but where's the harm in that? I'd like to talk to him. You think this idea of mine is nuts. Maybe it is. But if I could talk to this Von Ziegler guy, maybe he'd give me some advice."

Ellen pricked her finger on a thin shard of glass

and sucked at the bubble of blood accumulating on the tip. "Advice? I'll give you all the advice you need. Forget this ridiculous idea! Whoever heard of such a thing?"

The words were out of her mouth and she couldn't take them back. For an entire year, she'd never said it, vowing she'd let Judy reach this conclusion for herself. Now it was out in the open. She reached for Judy's hand. "I'm sorry, honey, I didn't mean to say that. But at least you know how I feel."

"You're really spooked, aren't you?" Judy stated quietly.

"I'm older than you are. It comes with the territory. Just promise me you'll try to forget about it, okay?"

One thing she didn't want to do was lie to Ellen, particularly now.

"Okay, Auntie," she said softly. "I'll try. But I won't promise." But she couldn't lie to herself either. Her mind was already made up.

Nine

The saddle of her bike was still damp with the morning's dew when Judy climbed aboard and rolled it toward the center of the parking lot. Ellen had gone to a farm nearby where the corn they harvested late in August was always sweet and tender. Harry was in the kitchen, wondering why the chopped meat he'd removed from the freezer early that morning still hadn't thawed.

She didn't want to do a lot of explaining about where she was going and what she was up to. This was the perfect moment. No one would even know she was gone.

When she reached the road that cut off Route 32 heading toward Rhinelander, Judy turned in and gunned her engine. The surface was paved, but bumpy, and from the amount of loose dirt and gravel collected at the side, it wasn't traveled very often. She was having fun bumping along when quite unexpectedly, she discovered a massive wrought-iron gate linking sections of a high stone wall. The closer she came, the more certain she was that the gates were the same design as the ones where she picked up that kid a few days earlier.

This must be another entrance to the estate, she thought, as she slowed her bike for a closer look. There were two great lion heads encircled in iron in the center of each gate. Attached to one gate was a rusty chain with a huge lock dangling from one end. The gate was open.

Judy rode closer for a better look, then gave the gate a shove. It creaked and swung slowly inward.

She listened to see if there was someone anywhere about. The air was heavy and still. A twig snapped and she whirled about, but no one was there. With a determined set to her jaw, she rolled the bike through the gates. Should she cut the engine? she wondered. No. This was the moment she'd been waiting for. There was no reason to apologize for being there or try to sneak around the property. She was here to meet Hans Von Ziegler and that's all there was to that. He certainly wouldn't write any letters of recommendation for some timid little thing who was too afraid to let him know what it really was she wanted.

She pushed off and headed up the drive. Both sides were lined with giant pines whose branches reached across the narrow roadway forming a majestic kind of arch. Suddenly the wind picked up and she realized she must be getting near the river. Her heart began to pound, but she wasn't quite sure why.

The drive began to narrow; it took a sharp turn, and she realized she must be at the back end of the estate. The roar of the bike's engine had begun to sound intrusive. If this Hans Von Ziegler liked living up here, alone and undisturbed, she wasn't likely to make a very good first impression. She brought the bike to a halt and killed the motor. It was a heavy old thing, but she'd push it the rest of the way, she decided. At least if she met this Von Ziegler guy before she got to the house, he'd know she didn't mean to be intrusive.

The size and magnitude of the great stone mansion that began to reveal itself beyond the trees was far more than she expected. It was more like a feudal castle that sat on the edge of a cliff high above the river that was snaking its way through the countryside.

In earlier days, this must have been a showplace, Judy thought. Instantly, she began to picture the Von Zieglers cavorting about on their mossy green lawns, coaxing giant lions and tigers through the paces of their circus repertoire.

The closer she came, the more undeniable the impression there were no signs of life here at all. What should she do next?

Facing the river was a formal portico with double oak doors. To one side was a round-handled bell. She gave it a pull. There was no sound. She pulled it again. Still nothing.

"Hello!" she heard herself call out. "Is anyone here?"

The only response was the sound her own voice made echoing off the stone walls. She roamed along the massive front of the building, trying to catch a glimpse of something, anything, through its large glass windows. Yet too much dirt and grime had caked on over the years to allow any view inside.

At the back, what once had been formal gardens

had long since been defeated by a repeated invasion of weeds.

She was on the verge of concluding that Hans Von Ziegler was little more than a figment of local hysteria and imagination when she discovered a man standing directly in front of her. Despite herself, she let out a startled cry.

The man thrust his hand forward shyly. "Er, may I help you?" he asked, then averted his gaze nervously.

By this time, Judy had recovered sufficiently to explain her reason for being there.

"I'd hoped to meet the owner of this house," she said quietly. "I'm extremely interested in the world of the circus and I understand that he might be able to help me."

"What sort of help do you require?" the man asked, still appearing very ill at ease.

"It would sound stupid to anyone else," she began. "Do you know where I could find Mr. Von Ziegler or when he might be here?"

"Yes. I am he."

It wasn't the answer she was expecting, and Judy was afraid her face revealed her disappointment. She'd better talk fast, she decided. "Oh, Mr. Von Ziegler! I'm so sorry. I mean, I didn't mean to intrude. I mean, I think you know what I mean." So far, she was having trouble getting her point across, but this was hardly the madman people in town spread such rumors about. He was so shy she actually felt a little sorry for him. She could scarcely believe the next words that came from her mouth. "I must have picked a terrible time. Maybe I should come back later."

"Not at all," he almost shouted in response. "Please

stay. It's very hot. I'll get us some lemonade."

Before she could stop him, he had run through a small side door and moments later emerged with folding table under one arm and two folding plastic chairs. He smiled a little self-consciously at her over his shoulder as he began to set them up, then ducked back inside again. The next time he appeared, it was with a tray carrying a tall icy pitcher of lemonade and two glasses.

"Let me help you," she insisted, lifting the glasses from the tray and setting them on the table. "This is what I do for a living."

He seemed not to notice what she said as he began to pour with one hand and indicated the chair in which she should sit with the other. "This is my own special recipe," he confided. "I hope you like it."

He was trying so hard to please her, Judy vowed she'd smile and lick her lips, even if it tasted like piss. "You must have known I was coming." She smiled ingratiatingly, not sure how long to keep up the small talk before stating the true purpose of her being there.

For his part, Hans was lost in thought. How long had he dreamed of living a normal life, finding someone he could love, escaping the torturous existence he'd been forced to endure for so many years? This blonde dimpled creature who sat across from him smiling and sipping lemonade was the answer to his prayers. But did he have the courage?

"I feel very embarrassed all of a sudden," Judy admitted out loud. "I had no business barging in on you like this."

"You believed what people say about me, didn't you?" He caught her completely off guard. "You thought there was a crazy man up here in this big house. If he's as crazy as people say, perhaps he won't mind or even care."

"Not at all," Judy protested. "I only wanted to talk with you. Some people advised against it, but I wanted to see for myself."

"And what do you see, if I may ask?"

So far, this wasn't the conversation Judy planned, but he was trying hard to be hospitable and she felt obligated to help him out.

"You're a little uncomfortable with me, but you're doing the best you can." She hadn't expected to be that blunt, but he seemed to take it okay.

"Yes. You see, I don't entertain very often."

If this was his idea of "entertaining," Judy thought, no wonder he didn't get a chance to do it often. "The lemonade is wonderful," she said and hoped she sounded sincere.

"I discourage people from coming here because I need privacy for my work," he went on.

"Your work?" It certainly wasn't landscaping or housekeeping, Judy decided with a quick glance around.

"My cats."

This was more like it, she thought. "You keep cats?"

"I paint them. I have rooms and rooms, filled with my work; some of it is very large. You see, my mother and father were with the circus. On canvas, I have re-created their lives."

"How interesting!" That sounded too eager, she told herself, but she was dying to have him invite her inside to see the paintings. Then she could draw him out about his mother and father, the people they'd worked with, and once she had his confidence, she could reveal her plans. "Maybe someday you'll show them to me?"

"What is your name?" he asked abruptly.

"Judy. Judy McAuliffe."

"Very pretty."

"Thank you."

"When my paintings are ready, I hope to have a grand exhibition. With the profits, I will try to make sense of my life."

Nothing Judy had heard about this man prepared her for the creature who sat on the other side of the little folding table staring off into space. "Do you have photographs?" she inquired.

"Some." Without another word, he rose and went back inside. Moments later, he returned with a fistful of dog-eared black-and-white snapshots. "These are my mother and father," he began. "They are Ilse and Klaus Von Ziegler."

In the photo, Ilse and Klaus were in the center ring. It was taken as they put some of the cats through their paces. Another looked as though it was taken at the finale. In the middle were Ilse and Klaus with six lions seated obediently on perches directly behind them. Off to one side was a towheaded young boy, in a costume that was a smaller version of the one Klaus wore. Judy looked closer and realized it was Hans, yet there was something puzzling about him. Despite all the bravura captured in the photograph, young Hans looked terrified.

What surprised her even more was the last snapshot in the batch. She stared at it transfixed. The boy was a teenager now, standing center ring, six lions on their platforms behind him. But a single beast clawed threateningly at the whip he held in his hand. Something in the boy's eyes sent a shiver down her spine.

"Amazing," Judy stated when she realized he'd been staring at her now for quite a while. "You look so different." She held the photo up for him to see.

He studied it for several moments. "That's because I am different," he told her. "This is not Hans. He is Horst."

"Well, of course," she exclaimed, looking from one photo to another. "You're twins. What fun! I always wanted to be a twin when I was a kid."

"It's not all 'fun,' as you put it," he said. "Horst was the animal trainer they expected us both to be. I had fear, like a hot piece of coal, burning right here in the center of my chest."

"You were very brave, just the same," she told him.

"Brave?" He spat the word as if it were something dirty. "Look at those eyes," he demanded, pointing to the picture of the younger boy with an accusing finger.

"But you did it just the same."

"Yes, I did. I got in the ring with those loathsome creatures because I had an even greater fear of Ilse and Klaus. Then, one day they were killed . . ." his voice trailed off and he shook his head absently.

Judy wasn't sure whether she should speak or not. She sat riveted to her seat and waited.

Hans began to rock back and forth, staring blindly into space. Moments later, he straightened up and seemed in better control of himself. "More lemonade?" he asked.

"I've had plenty," Judy assured him, now certain she'd overstayed her welcome. "I shouldn't have stayed this long, but to tell the truth, I wanted to meet you. Maybe we can do this again." She rose, not sure whether he would try to follow her or not. "Does your brother live here, too?" she asked, hoping she hadn't asked too much already.

"Sometimes."

"Maybe I can meet him too, one day. I'd like that."

"I wouldn't!" he snapped and began to massage his left temple. "I am sorry," he apologized quickly. "I must ask you to leave right away. I'm getting a terrible headache."

She was almost running as she headed for the bike. "It's my fault. I stayed too long. I promise I won't next time!" She was astride the bike before he reached her, gave the accelerator a deft stomp with her foot, threw the bike in gear, and bumped her way toward the long drive that headed back to the county road. For a split second, she wondered what she'd do if she found the gate had been locked in the meantime.

A wave of relief washed over her as she neared the gate and noticed it stood half open, then found herself thinking about the kid from the grocery store she'd picked up in front of the estate on another road. Poor kid was scared out of his wits, she thought. In fact, she was starting to feel a little uneasy herself, but she wasn't quite sure why.

Ten

Horst was furious. That fool would ruin everything. He knew what Hans was planning and he had to work fast.

The new cats were still groggy from the sedatives delivered by the stun gun he had to use in order to get them into their cages. The dark cat was a beauty; the lighter-colored one lacked the smooth, sleek lines he preferred, but with training she could join the group he used to dress the ring. Their performance was unextraordinary, but their mere presence lent a grandeur to the spectacle he was creating.

On hot days like this one, the high leather boots resisted as he tried to pull them on. He stopped a moment between tugs and found himself thinking about the pretty blonde thing sipping lemonade with Hans shortly before.

Could this be his Felidia?

Hans had pretended that Horst was nowhere around. He knew that. And he knew what Hans was thinking. Clearly, he'd have to punish him again. The fool had not understood a thing. When would he learn he could never escape? And certainly never with a pretty young thing Horst had chosen for himself.

This time, the boot slid on more easily and he jammed his foot into the other. Luckily he'd gained no weight over the years, so the boots, though decades old, still fit him.

The twill jodhpurs were threadbare at the knees and threatened to give away completely. He made a mental note to have Hans patch them one day soon before they became unusable. He loved these jodhpurs. They'd belonged to his father. They were part of the costume he wore whenever he rehearsed the act, and had been the gift of a white hunter when Klaus and Ilse were on safari in Africa before the start of World War II.

He stood before the long mirror carefully examining the reflection as he buttoned the white silk shirt. His wheat-colored hair was beginning to thin and turning slightly gray at the temples, but the rich pomade he used as part of his theatrical makeup still managed to turn back the calendar with reasonable success. He considered applying just a dollop before heading below-stairs to fetch his cats, then decided against it.

This was only a practice session, after all. He would definitely use a touch of pomade when Hans's young friend returned to visit.

The stench of animal feces and urine never failed to take his breath away as he moved through the cavernous basement among the locked cages.

The black bitch he'd just captured cowered in a corner and peered fearfully through the bars when he lit the overhead bulb that began to swing to and fro in front of her cage. He liked a beast with a little fight and had frankly expected more from this one. Perhaps the sedative had been too powerful. Occasionally, he'd miscalculated the proper dosage, and until he learned not to be so heavyhanded, several of the cats had died.

Once Hans learned not to be so squeamish, he had become quite a good butcher. The cats were skinned and whole sections of their carcasses were placed in the giant freezer upstairs just off the kitchen. Later Hans would carve them up, boil the meat, and create quite a nourishing stew to feed the other cats. The system was quite efficient, actually.

The bare light bulb continued its swinging motion and made it difficult for Horst to insert his key into the large padlock at the end of the heavy chain that secured the gate on one side of the cage. At last, it slipped into place, the lock clicked open, and he slid the heavy chain from the bars.

The animal whimpered and cried in the corner.

"Stop that!" he screamed, delivering the back of his hand across its nose. Seconds later the nose spurted blood. He'd have to toughen this one up, he decided. A sleek, black cat always looked good among the lighter-colored others, but it must have spirit. Otherwise, what good was it? A cat without spirit might just as well end its days upstairs in Hans's deep freezer.

He grabbed the beast by the long mane and shoved it toward the gate. Another pull and it fell to the floor in a heap. He grabbed at the long hair once again, gave it a twist, and pulled a studded metal collar from a hook on his belt. Once secured, he dragged the animal up a flight of narrow steps at one end of the basement.

At the top of the steps, he threw back a heavy iron bolt that held the doors shut. A carved wooden door swung open and Horst pulled the beast after him into a room that had once been the grand ballroom of the Von Ziegler mansion.

In the middle of the room was a huge circus ring, isolated from the outer reaches of the high-ceilinged chamber by tall bars to deny the performing animals any route of escape.

With the leather lead attached to her collar in one hand and a long bullwhip in the other, Horst paraded the new cat around the perimeter of the ring. The moment she slowed her pace or looked the slightest bit reluctant to continue, the whip cracked. She screamed in pain again and again, but Horst knew she would remember her lessons well. Few forgot this first day. He wished Hans could have been trained as easily.

An hour or so later, the animal was his. She was as docile as a kitten and responded to the slightest flick of the whip. She leapt from perch to perch with graceful agility, then posed prettily on the last, back on her haunches, front paws tucked together under her chin. There was a trace of dried blood beneath her nose from the blow she received earlier, but otherwise, her first day of training had gone extremely well.

Horst extended his hand beneath the nose of the

sleek black cat. Its animal instinct knew what was expected. It purred, then licked the back of Horst's hand, then stared into his eyes for approval. He patted the black mane he'd treated so threateningly before.

A satisfied smile began to form at the corners of his lips. With luck, the new act might be ready earlier than he ever dared to dream.

If only he had his Felidia.

Ellen was flitting from table to table, placing fan-shaped napkins between knives and forks at the center of the Rathskeller placemats. Behind the bar, Harry wrestled a case of whiskey toward the storage compartment at the far end. When Judy suddenly appeared, they both forgot what they were doing and stared.

"Hi," she said, as breezily as she could, knowing what was sure to follow.

"Where have you been?" Ellen demanded with no attempt to disguise anger or concern.

"Visiting," she replied and hurried toward the bar to give Harry a hand with the whiskey bottles.

"Oh, no you don't," Ellen shouted, following right behind.

When Judy turned back, her face was a study in cherubic innocence. "Is something the matter?"

Controlling her exasperation wasn't easy, but on the other hand, Ellen was so glad to see her niece she could have kissed her. Anyway, she was going to give it her best shot.

"Judy," she began. "Your timing stinks, if you must know. We made a bargain when you came here that I'd give you plenty of space. I trusted you and I still do, but we're all very nervous these days. You just plain disappeared this morning and that's not like you."

In a flash, she was around the bar, giving Ellen a reassuring hug. "I'm sorry, Ellen, honestly. I just had some things I had to do and they took longer than I expected. I should have left you a note. I will the next time, okay?"

From where he stood behind the bar, Harry was unconvinced. She was up to something. He prayed whatever it was didn't involve any more conversations with Officer Jim Sweeney. Or his brother. Law and Order, he thought, and just thinking about them gave him chills.

When Judy turned away, she glanced in the mirror behind the bar and discovered Ellen still watching her. Ellen knew where she'd been, but she wasn't saying anything. That was cool, Judy thought. She wanted to reassure her aunt that Hans Von Ziegler wasn't someone she need worry about, but, for the time being, the subject had been dropped. She decided maybe it was better to leave it that way.

Around nine o'clock when there was a lull after dinner, Ellen went to the kitchen. Harry was mopping countertops, deep in thought. She watched him wordlessly for a moment, then asked, "Can I have a cigarette?"

He jumped, then spun around. "Holy shit, you scared me. How long have you been standing there?"

"I love watching a man hard at work."

"It's a rotten habit. I don't want you to pick it up again."

"One cigarette isn't a habit."

"Goddam that kid. I wish she'd just call her mother and let us all off the hook!"

"I hope it's as simple as that."

Harry pulled a pack of cigarettes from his shirt pocket, put two of them in his mouth, and lit them both. He handed one of them to Ellen. "Just like the movies," he grinned.

"With or without a happy ending?"

He slid his arm around her waist, then ran his hand over her buttocks, giving them a firm, affectionate squeeze. "Speaking of endings, this one's about as good as they get."

She looked deep into the dark brown eyes she'd loved since the first time she saw him and for a fleeting moment forgot all about Trudy Kraus, her missing daughter and a niece with lunatic notions about joining the circus.

The pay phone must have rung at least six times before Judy realized Ellen was nowhere around. She was sure, by the time she answered it, whoever was calling would have given up.

"Rathskeller," she shouted into the mouthpiece, not sure she could be heard above the din of the jukebox.

"I would like to speak with Miss Judy McAuliffe," the voice at the other end said somewhat stiffly.

"That's me," she replied. "Who's this?"

"Miss McAuliffe, I am Horst Von Ziegler."

"You're who?" she shouted again into the phone, not believing what she just heard.

"Von Ziegler. Horst. My brother has told me all about you."

"No kidding," she beamed. "How about that?" Quite unexpectedly, she was lost for words.

"My brother has told me of your interest in our family, is that correct?"

Judy looked furtively around. Ellen was still out of sight. "Yeah," she said, placing one hand over the phone. "I'm very interested."

"Then please visit us again sometime soon," came the reply.

Again, Judy looked over her shoulder. She knew she had to talk fast. "I'd love to. When?"

There was a pause at the other end of the line before he spoke again. "I must make some preparations. Often I travel on very short notice, but I will phone you again very soon."

"I work nights," she added hastily. "But some morning or afternoon would be perfect."

"Very soon," he repeated, then broke the connection.

Judy still had the receiver in her hand when she saw Ellen coming through the kitchen door. She shrugged and put the phone back on its hook. "Wrong number," she lied and wished she hadn't.

If only Kathy Kraus would show up, Judy yearned. Then she'd have a perfect excuse for taking off suddenly in the middle of the day. She could spend an hour or so with Kathy as well as spend a couple of hours with Horst and no one need be any the wiser. But Kathy was still missing.

She began to wonder if Bud Mosher would cover for her, then rejected the idea almost as soon as it formed. Bud was always looking for convincing arguments to keep her in town. He wasn't a likely accomplice in her scheme. No one in Ruttenburg ever seemed to travel far from home and Labor Day weekend was no exception. Trudy Kraus had run her tail off serving customers, despite the fact that she felt a lot of them had stopped by the Rathskeller just to see how she was holding up. She was more an object of curiosity than concern, but Trudy chose to ignore the fact and carry on with her duties as best she knew how.

The bar was filled with Rathskeller regulars when the pay phone began to ring just before midnight. This time, Judy didn't wait for Ellen to answer it. She pushed through a tight cluster of locals heatedly debating who would win the American League pennant.

"Rathskeller," she announced, shouting into the mouthpiece.

At first, there was no reply, but Judy could hear someone breathing at the other end.

"Stony Creek Rathskeller," she repeated, trying to make herself heard over the din of the noisy bar.

A soft voice responded at last, but it was hard to hear. *"Fräulein McAuliffe, bitte . . ."*

"Speaking!" she yelled.

"Ah, good." The voice was louder now. "I am Horst Von Ziegler."

Judy stole a glance over her shoulder to be certain no one was within earshot. "My God!" she exclaimed. *"The* Horst Von Ziegler?" She couldn't contain her excitement.

"There is no other, Fräulein," he replied stiffly. "I

do not wish to intrude on your work . . ."

"It's no intrusion," she shot back, not wanting him to get away.

"Could you make time to pay me a brief visit, say, tomorrow?"

"Could I! Wow!" Judy answered breathlessly.

"Tomorrow, then, if you are able."

Judy caught her breath and her heart began to pound. At last she was making progress. "I'd love to!" she sighed happily.

"May I expect you around noon?"

"I can't wait!"

"Good. It is settled," said Horst, then added softly, "Normally I discourage visitors. So, Fräulein, please keep this our little secret."

Her body tingled with anticipation as she replaced the receiver.

Eleven

The heat wave was still unbroken; and as Judy sped along the back road toward the Von Ziegler estate, her motorcycle kicked up a heavy cloud of dust.

When she reached the front gate, one side stood slightly ajar.

That's good, she thought. He's still expecting me. In reality she was afraid he might suddenly change his mind.

She climbed off the bike and pushed it through the gate, making sure to leave the gate in the same position it was in when she arrived.

The day was blisteringly hot but she felt a sudden chill as she climbed back on the bike and made her way up the drive. Once the massive stone mansion came into view, it looked, as it had on her earlier visit, utterly desolate and abandoned.

At least she didn't have to hide her bike, like the kid from the grocery store. She was an invited guest. That was pretty special, even if half the things she'd heard were true.

Moments before she reached the imposing carved wooden doors that were the formal entrance to the main building of the estate, one of them swung open. Hans Von Ziegler stood just inside, framed in darkness.

It wasn't until she moved up the steps that Judy noticed he seemed to have several days' growth of beard. On his forehead were several bruises. His hand clearly trembled when he reached to take her arm as she entered the dimly lit foyer.

"I'm glad you could take time from your duties to visit me again," he offered, opening another door and indicating that she should follow.

"I told your brother that morning or afternoon would be fine," Judy replied. "I don't have much to do until happy hour." Hans looked perplexed. "You know, cocktail time. Beer and backups would be more like it."

"Ah, yes," he answered, but he was clearly not paying attention.

Something about him was beginning to alarm her. "Your brother phoned me," she felt obligated to explain. "I guess you must have told him how I was hoping to get some information or make some contacts with circus people." She heard herself give a nervous little laugh, but she wasn't quite sure why.

"He seems to know everything. It wasn't necessary for me to tell him."

Judy didn't have the faintest idea what that was supposed to mean. She just wished that Horst would appear and put an end to this conversation. Judy began to remember the weird things she'd heard about this man that she'd chosen to ignore. But then she thought about the afternoon they'd spent together on the lawn sipping lemonade. No doubt about it. He was a little schitzy, she decided.

"If it's not a good time, I could always come back later," she suggested.

"Oh, no!" he insisted. "This is just fine. May I get you some tea?"

"What about your brother? Shouldn't we wait for him?"

Hans began to shake his head like a schoolboy who couldn't remember something he thought he memorized only the day before. "I'm so forgetful lately. I'm afraid it's the headaches, of course, but that's still no excuse for bad manners."

Judy regarded him quizzically, but then, without a word, he left the room. She hadn't really looked at her surroundings until she realized that at least for the moment she was completely alone.

Heavy drapes covered the tall windows, allowing only the slimmest rays of light to pass. Judy was tempted to yank back the drapes to get a better look around but quickly decided against it. She was, after all, a guest in this house. Once Horst appeared, she was certain he would correct the situation himself without any help from her.

There was a small Victorian settee positioned just in front of the windows, and in the dim light it looked as though it might be covered with a dark wine-colored horsehair. Two carved straight-backed chairs stood by a small fireplace with a round table between them in front of the hearth. If Horst were to join them for tea, they could move the whole arrangement over to the settee, Judy mused, wishing he'd arrive before she began to feel even more jittery than she already did.

She could hear sounds coming from a long way off. Footsteps, then nothing more for several minutes. She moved about the room, then peeked through the parted drapes to the bright, blinding sunlight outdoors. When she closed them again a sprinkle of dust fell like the start of a winter snowstorm. It was stuffy in the room, although not as hot as it was outside. For a moment, she thought she heard someone outside the door. She turned, not knowing who she was about to see, but her anticipation was only met by other sounds even further away.

Was it her imagination or had she heard the scream of some wild jungle beast?

If only that were so. If Horst Von Ziegler was training his animals for an imminent return to the circus, she'd better talk pretty convincingly if she hoped to be considered as a member of his entourage. Was it possible she could be that lucky?

Obviously, Hans liked her. Maybe she could get him to speak to his brother on her behalf. Why not? Lots of crazier things happened all the time.

She never heard him enter the room. When she turned, there he was in full costume, right down to the shiny black boots and bullwhip in his hand. Judy was so excited she was afraid to speak.

"Fräulein," he said simply, clicking his booted heels and making a theatrical bow from the waist. "I hope I haven't kept you waiting."

"Are you kidding?" Judy asked, still wide-eyed. "I'd have waited all day." She knew she was grinning like a half-wit, but she couldn't help herself.

With yet another theatrical gesture, he indicated she should be seated on the Victorian settee in front of the windows. "I had hoped Hans would have prepared tea for us, but as usual, he has failed me."

"It's my fault," she insisted, wanting nothing to spoil the relationship she might depend on very soon. "He's been very kind, really."

Horst was striding about the room slapping the palm of one hand with the coiled bullwhip he held in the other. "Simple-minded would be more accurate, but that's not what we're here to talk about, is it, young Fräulein?"

"I really appreciate this," she said, wondering how best to launch the conversation. "I guess you know why I wanted to talk to you so badly."

He turned to face her unexpectedly. "Stand, please." She did as she was told. "Turn." She did. "Excellent. For once, he's done something right."

"He's very nice."

" 'Nice,' as you put it, is not good enough, Fräulein."

This wasn't going the way she'd hoped. Judy decided that from this point on, she'd let him do the talking.

He stared at her for several moments, without saying a word. "Sit," he commanded, at last.

The horsehair sofa scratched the back of her thighs and Judy wished she'd worn something more protective than the khaki shorts she'd pulled on earlier that morning. But she had good legs; they were long, shapely, and tan. And good legs were an important part of the picture she hoped to present. It was important for Horst to be able to perceive all the physical attributes she had going for her, and as quickly as possible.

The sofa was hard and uncomfortable, but Judy knew she'd have felt uncomfortable anyway. Horst stood on the far side of the small room staring at her in the half-light that came from the small opening in the heavy drapes. She could barely make out his face from where she sat, but it was obvious that Horst and Hans were identical twins. What amazed her was that their personalities were so entirely different.

Then, from somewhere deep in the bowels of the vast stone edifice, came another piercing cry like the one she'd heard before.

Horst stiffened visibly, as if alerted to some unexpected danger.

"What was that?" Judy asked brightly, hoping this might be a way to get the conversation around to animals, the circus, and all the things she'd hoped they would talk about.

The cry came again, then another. But the sounds were from such a distance it was hard to tell what kind of animal had made them.

Horst began to pace. "Fool!" he snapped, causing Judy to flinch involuntarily. For several moments, Horst seemed unaware of her presence. His mood was darkening as she sat completely motionless, fearful now that an intrusion of any kind would only make things worse.

But this was her big moment. She was certain that Horst Von Ziegler was readying his circus act on this very property. Somehow, she had to convince him to involve her in the process. She had a lot to learn, but she was ready to do whatever was required. The main thing was to not lose the opportunity to make a good impression while she was here.

It had begun to sound like a chorus of animals shrieking from the depths below. The sounds were faint but insistent.

At last, Horst turned and acknowledged her presence once again. "You see, Fräulein, this is what happens when imbeciles are allowed to function in places where they don't belong. Years of training and effort can be destroyed with the blink of an eye. Especially when the eye does not see things as clearly as it should."

"Is there anything I can do to help?" she asked. She knew she had to choose her words carefully, but this was the opening she'd been waiting for.

"Not yet," he snapped. "You will wait here until I return." With that, he slid the thick wooden panel that separated this chamber from a larger one beyond and disappeared into the dim light of the cavernous room beyond. For a long while, she could hear the steady pounding of his heavy boots on the wooden floor. Then, there was silence.

Judy strained her ears for any sound that might alert her as to what was happening. And where was Hans while all of this was going on? Horst was clearly very angry and Judy began to fear for Hans's safety. None of this was any of her business, but she began to see herself as some kind of diplomatic mediary; a peacemaker between the two brothers.

She smiled at the thought. That was the answer. She must find Hans and tell him of the plan that was starting to form at the back of her mind.

Horst had neglected to close the sliding panel when he left the room. Judy rose and crossed to the open doorway. She stood stock-still on its threshold, alert to any sound that might warn her of Horst's sudden return.

Nothing.

And Hans could be anywhere in this vast structure. Perhaps he was painting. That might account for the almost-palpable silence that had now occurred.

Hesitantly, Judy began to tiptoe first through one room, then another. Each was as heavily draped as the one in which she and Horst had their first brief interview.

Unsure what it was that led her there, Judy found herself suddenly standing amid stacks of canvases and tubes of paint. Dozens of brushes were scattered about the room, some strewn about on the floor, some placed carefully in glass jars or coffee tins. This was the only room she'd seen so far with no heavy drape covering its window.

One by one, she examined the paintings. One stack had nothing but golden lions with heavy gilded manes that seemed to explode from the canvas. Another depicted menacing black-and-amber-striped tigers with glistening, needle-pointed fangs. There were jaundice-eyed panthers that made her shiver with an unexpected chill she couldn't comprehend.

Then came the slow awareness that probably many of the species portrayed here on canvas actually lived somewhere in the hidden depths of the estate.

A beast screamed again. It was closer now. Without thinking, Judy whirled about and followed its sound, then it stopped. She found herself hurrying toward the back end of the house. There was still no sign of Hans and secretly she was glad. Without realizing it, she'd decided to make her move. It was time to inform Horst that she knew about his plans and that she wanted to be a part of them. Who knew if she'd ever get this chance again?

In the kitchen, she found a door slightly ajar that clearly led to a lower level. With no one around to prevent her, Judy began to move down a dark and creaking flight of wooden steps. A very dim light some distance away barely allowed her to make her way to the bottom without taking a serious fall. Halfway down the steps, she'd already become dizzy from the unmistakable stench of animal waste.

At the bottom of the steps, it took a moment for her eyes to adjust to the absence of light. As she peered about, she realized she was in a huge, vaultlike chamber, carved from the rock on which the mansion had been built. A heavy iron gate separated this chamber from another beyond it. Judy thought it looked like the entrance to a vast, underground prison.

The walls of the second chamber were lined with huge, caged wagons, the kind of vehicles used in the heyday of the circus.

The wagons had heavy, wooden-spoked wheels and were painted a shiny red, trimmed with fancy gilt scrollwork. In cages like these, lions, tigers, leopards, and all manner of wild animals would be paraded through the streets of town on the way to the fairgrounds where circus tents were raised and waiting for the show to begin.

Heart pounding with excitement, Judy moved from this chamber into the next. Next to a wall was a pile of bones. Could this be all that was left of one of Horst's animals? She found herself wondering which one of them had died and what had caused it. No wonder it didn't survive, if they spent their lives caged in this musty dungeon. She'd discuss this with Horst later, once she knew she'd gained his confidence.

The closer she got to the light at the far end, the easier it became to distinguish her surroundings. There was a line of wagons in the next chamber, set one after another as though ready to begin the parade. As Judy approached, the wheels of the first one creaked and she realized some creature had begun to move about inside. She decided to sneak a little closer and have a peek.

Not wanting to disturb the animals, announcing to Horst that she'd disobeyed his orders to remain where he left her, Judy moved noiselessly to the edge of the cage and peered through its bars. Her heart froze in horror.

It was moments before her eyes connected with her brain and still she didn't believe the message they had sent. Inside the cage, peering back at her, were the crazed and red-rimmed eyes, not of a captured wild beast, but of a human being. A young woman, on hands and knees, was ravenously devouring the contents of a small bowl that had been placed before her on the floor.

It had to be some kind of ghastly, cruel mistake!

Judy ran from cage to cage, desperately pleading with her own mind to end this ghoulish hoax and allow her to see the animals she knew were there before this insane flight of imagination took place. But what she saw was unspeakable horror. Cage after cage of tethered women with hair matted and filthy, fingernails broken and blackened like claws.

It was the sight of Kathy Kraus, naked and unconscious, hanging by her wrists from the ceiling of a cell hewn from the rocky foundation, that caused Judy to shriek in revulsion and stumble blindly from chamber to chamber, seeking the cellar steps and safety of the world beyond.

Twelve

Her breath came in raw, ragged gasps, but the horror of what she'd just witnessed kept her going. A searing pain pierced the center of her chest, but she plunged on.

She had stumbled twice racing up the steps from the basement and her shins were badly scraped. Miraculously, she'd made her way back through the house, out the front door, and into the blinding sunlight. But when she ran to the spot where she'd left her bike, she discovered it was gone!

There was no time to think or try to figure things out. All she knew was that she had to get away from there as fast as she could. The image of Kathy Kraus hanging by her wrists swinging to and fro as she dangled from the ceiling prevented her from stopping for even a split second to catch her breath.

If she could somehow get back to the road, she might be able to stop a car, the same way the kid from the grocery store had flagged her down. The important thing was not to be seen beforehand. Horst must have heard her scream. Hans, too, wherever he was.

They'd scared the wits out of the grocery boy and all he did was watch them from across the road. Imagine what they'd do to someone who'd discovered their hideous secret!

If she could lose herself in the wooded property that surrounded the estate, she might make it back to the road before either one of them could find her.

Tears stung her cheeks and blinded her vision as she thrashed through the defiant underbrush that seemed determined to hold her back.

Then, without warning, there was a thunderous crack as the earth gave way beneath her feet and Judy felt herself plummeting through space. She landed with an explosive thud that knocked the air from her lungs and left her unconscious.

When she finally opened her eyes, it was almost dark. As she gradually regained her senses, she was becoming more and more frightened. She was on the verge of hysteria when somewhere in the back of her mind, a deeper instinct, demanded that she fight it off. If she gave in now, she was lost.

In the waning light, she could see she was at the bottom of a deep pit. She couldn't call for help or one of them would surely find her. Not since her mother died had she felt so completely and utterly alone, with nothing but her wits to save her. She rolled her eyes toward the heavens more in desperation than in prayer and spotted the thin, gray protrusion of a network of roots extending from the earth just above her head. If she could get a firm hold of one of them, she might be able to pull herself up and out of there to freedom.

116

It took several unsuccessful tries, and just when she was almost too exhausted to try again, she leapt in the air, grabbed hold of one of the roots, and hung on with all the strength she could muster. It held, even with her full weight dangling from it. The root must have been attached at both ends to some living plant-life growing nearby. Suddenly, Judy found herself thinking it was like hanging onto one of those devices attached to walls to support the handicapped.

Somehow, she managed to grab it with both hands at the same time, kicking toeholds into the loose earth below her to support her feet. She knew she was working against time as she inched her way upward to another cluster of roots protruding above her.

She managed to get a grip on that one, too, and tugged at it with one hand to make sure it wouldn't pull away on her. It, too, held firm and once again she made her way slowly upward. She grunted as she inched her way toward the edge of the pit. Dirt and pebbles fell down on her, raining dust in her eyes. She blinked fiercely to clear her vision.

Reaching blindly above her for something else to grab and oblivious to the pain in her hands, her breath came in wheezing gasps. But slowly, inch by inch, the climb was paying off.

It worked. The root system was holding firm and Judy was able to dig her toes into soft dirt at the sides of the pit. It was a slow and arduous climb. With each new victory, she paused to catch her breath and save her strength.

For a moment, she was unaware she'd reached the

top, and discovered she'd reached the edge only as she flailed about for anything she could hang onto that might help keep her moving upward. She felt her strength slipping away when she tried to haul herself over the rim of the excavation. She dug her elbows into the ground and looked about anxiously. Judy was drenched with sweat when she finally raised her head over the edge for a quick look around, alert to any sound in the woods announcing Hans or Horst might be somewhere close-by.

Her head and shoulders were out and she groped desperately for something to hold while she flung one leg over the side.

Fingers clutching at the dry ground, she felt a tidal wave of exhaustion wash over her. She was beginning to slide, slowly at first, then faster and faster. She kicked at the wall of the pit, hoping to find a spot that would allow her to dig her toes back in to prevent the ever-quickening slide. The dirt beneath her started to crumble. Desperately, she flailed about, clutching for anything within reach that might have stopped the fall that sent her free-falling through space to the bottom of the pit.

By the time she caught her breath, she was trembling with fatigue. The sky above was pitch black, and tiny stars had begun to gleam in the few patches of sky still visible between the imposing pines that stood like sentinels above. Now and then they swayed and creaked in the light summer wind.

At daybreak, she would try again.

Once again Judy found herself confronted by the image of Kathy Kraus, hanging naked, like a fatted calf waiting to be slaughtered.

Oh, my God! she suddenly thought. What if it was true? Was it possible this madman nourished his prized "cats" with the flesh of the others? The thought made her gag and with it came the unexpected realization that she was horrifyingly accurate.

Groping the earthen walls that surrounded her, she found a place that was smooth enough to lean against and hold her up as she sank to a seated position. If she ever expected to escape this place, she had to get her strength back.

It was closing time at the Rathskeller and Bud Mosher was the only customer left at the bar. He wanted to reassure Ellen that she had nothing to worry about, but when he tried, his words were unconvincing.

He'd begun with the possibility that Judy had pulled up stakes and headed south long before anyone expected.

That didn't work, because Ellen had already checked her room. She knew where Judy kept her money, and from time to time, she counted it. It wasn't something she was proud of doing, but it gave her a handle on how long Judy would stick around. By Ellen's count, she still had a pretty good wait. Furthermore, the money was still there. So were her clothes.

She'd left around noontime, without a word to anyone.

Ellen filled in behind the bar when dinner customers began to arrive and Harry was needed in the kitchen. When Bud showed up for happy hour, he sensed that something was wrong. It wasn't that Judy was late. Clearly, Ellen was very worried.

"Every time I look at Trudy, I nearly burst into tears," she told him quietly earlier in the evening. "I don't know why, Bud, but I'm scared."

For the first hour or so, it hadn't been so hard to try to kid her out of it. The later it got, the more concerned they all became. They were all grateful when the last of the evening's customers paid up and left the bar.

Finally, they could speak openly with each other.

Harry leaned against the back of the bar, tugged a cigarette from his breast pocket and lit it. He glanced over at Ellen. "Okay," he sighed, passing the cigarette to her and lighting another one for himself. "Just promise me when you see that niece of yours walk through the door, you won't give me those 'Come on, Harry, just one' looks ever again!"

She took the cigarette and inhaled deeply. "I called Jim Sweeney," she said in a voice that was barely audible.

"Has everyone gone fucking nuts around here?" Harry erupted, slamming his hand on the bar. It was enough to make Bud Mosher jump.

"We live in the age of computers, Harry," she said through tightly clenched teeth. "They plug those things in and they know things in an instant."

"Right."

"Well, that's why I did it," she retorted as though speaking to a slightly dense child. "If there were an accident of some kind . . ." She didn't finish her sentence.

Harry turned to Bud. "And if you had any balls, you'd have turned her head or some other part of her anatomy months ago and none of this would have happened."

Bud looked crestfallen. Harry said exactly what he'd been thinking all night.

Now it was Ellen's turn again. She looked from Harry to Bud and back again. "Come on, guys. We're all feeling the strain of this. If Kathy hadn't disappeared, we'd chalk this up to youth and hormones, have another drink, and go to bed. In the morning, everything would be back to normal."

Harry's voice was even now. "So what did young Officer Sweeney have to say?"

"Nothing."

"Nothing to say? Or nothing to report?"

"Both."

"I'm here almost every night," Bud added. "If she had anybody else paying close attention, I'd be the first to notice."

"And if the girl had any sense, she'd have thrown a hammerlock around your neck and we wouldn't be standing around here at midnight like a bunch of nervous Nellies."

"Harry, that doesn't help. We're all scared to death, so let's admit it and not go blaming each other or Judy or anyone else, okay?"

A pair of headlights shone through the big picture window in the dining room. All three were instantly alert. Then they receded, and their light disappeared. Someone had used the parking lot to turn around on the road outside.

For a long while after that, Ellen, Harry, and Bud

were left in silence with their own private thoughts.

The first light of day woke Judy from a fitful sleep. She stood and stretched with an aching stiffness that invaded her entire body. She was covered with thin lines of coagulated blood from the cuts and scrapes experienced the day before.

Above her was the hanging root she'd first clung to the previous night when her plans for escape had been so high. She stared at it in the morning light as though it were the enemy, an inanimate object that had betrayed her in a way she wasn't likely to forget.

Regardless, she was ready to begin again. First light came early in summer months. With any luck, she'd have herself out of there before Horst or Hans even awakened. She was suddenly filled with a giddy, unexplainable sense of hope.

Her mouth was still dry from the dust she'd swallowed and her heart began to pound. What was it she just heard?

Was it the sound of a motor? She listened and thought she heard the ground tremble, but she wasn't sure. The harder she listened, the less she was able to hear.

Then came a crackling sound. It was the rustling of leaves. Was it the wind blowing them about or was someone approaching?

Judy froze with fear.

Then came the distinct sound of approaching footsteps. She peered anxiously upward, praying that what she heard was an approaching hunter or someone seeking out a campsite, unaware they were on posted ground.

Suddenly, there he was, just as she'd seen him before, in full circus uniform. Incredibly cold blue eyes stared down at her. Judy felt herself go weak, then just as abruptly as he appeared, he vanished from the rim of the pit.

She thought she heard a car door slam. Or was it the truck that was parked by the side of the road when she rescued the boy from the grocery store?

It seemed like months ago that this goofy kid was standing in the middle of the road with his arms flailing like a semaphore. It had crossed her mind to leave him there. After all, she was already late for work. She wasn't sure if he was really in trouble or just goofing around, but something in his eyes as she sped past told her she'd better stop. Something was terribly wrong.

Was it ever!

Who would come speeding by and rescue her in her hour of need? Obviously, no one.

Thirteen

From where she stood at the bottom of the pit, Judy could only see his head and shoulders when Horst returned. He moved back and forth and seemed to be pulling something.

Suddenly, he turned, and without warning, she watched helplessly as a large net descended into the hole and enveloped her completely.

She screamed when it hit her, knocking her to the ground. It was permeated with a stench of urine so powerful she could hardly breathe.

From where Horst stood above her, he manipulated another rope that pulled the net close around her until she was trussed like a captured animal. Moments later, she felt herself being hauled upward.

Once out of the hole, Horst laid his captive on the ground beside it. Not far away, she could see a wooden cage perched on the back of the old pickup truck.

She was amazed at his pure brute strength as he hauled in the net that kept her captive, slung it over his shoulder, and headed for the back of the truck.

Then he sat her down on the tailgate and unlocked the cage.

She wanted to plead with him not to do this, to release her now, to let her go. But somewhere deep within, she knew this could only make things worse. At least for the time being she must not resist. Somehow she knew she must not even speak.

Once the cage was open, he pulled her free of the net, grabbed her by her long blonde hair, and pulled her to the barred entrance. With one powerful hand on the back of her head, he shoved her through the opening, then he slammed the cage door shut. She heard the metallic click of the lock that punctuated her captivity.

Inside the cage, there was almost no room to move. For a brief moment, Judy couldn't believe this was actually happening. Then once again came the image of poor Kathy Kraus and the others, penned up behind bars somewhere in the depths of the stone mansion on the hill.

No one in the world had any idea they were there. From the looks of several, they'd been imprisoned for a very long time.

Horst was rummaging around in the cab of the truck, and when he returned Judy saw that he was carrying a huge canvas tarp. Without a word, he dropped it over the cage and instantly she was plunged into darkness. And for the first time, she was overwhelmed with the sense of being utterly helpless and completely terrified.

The truck's engine began to cough and sputter and presently the vehicle rolled forward. Judy lay on her back and tried to kick the cage door open, but it was no use. As the truck picked up speed, it jerked and bounced over what she could only assume was unpaved terrain. When the ride finally smoothed out, she was convinced they were on the drive leading back to the mansion.

When they finally came to a halt, she heard the truck door slam, then footsteps in the gravel.

She blinked against the harsh sunlight when he slid the tarpaulin from her cage. She looked about, but wasn't quite sure where she was. Horst had busied himself with the lock and she began to wonder if, once the cage had been opened, she could possibly make a run for it. What she saw on his face was a look of such frightening determination, she decided against it. Without doubt, Hans was her only salvation. Where was he? she wondered.

When the cage door at last sprang open, her back and legs had become so stiff it was difficult to move.

With an unexpected gesture of sudden gallantry, Horst reached up and took her by the hand. As he helped her down from the tailgate of the truck, he bowed from the waist and clicked the heels of his boots.

"Welcome to the Circus Von Ziegler," he solemnly proclaimed. It was the first time he had spoken to her. She watched in dread as he removed a shiny silver collar with a long metallic chain from a bag attached to his waist. A small key protruded from the collar; he removed the key before he placed the collar around Judy's neck and snapped it shut. "Just a little restraining device," he smiled. "This way I can feel certain you will not try to run away."

He wound the chain around his hand until he had

a lead of five feet or so, then gave the chain a tug, causing Judy to stumble forward. He smiled again with obvious satisfaction.

This was the moment when Judy realized that if she did not obey him, he could snap her neck with a simple twist of his wrist.

He led her down a flight of stone steps at the rear of the mansion. From somewhere in the distance, Judy heard the muted cries of the others echoing through the cavernous recesses of the massive edifice.

For some reason, he was leading her away from them, Judy realized. Horst unlocked another door and led her through it. As they moved along the passage, she no longer heard the others, only the sound of their footsteps against the hard floor. They continued along the narrow corridor until they reached another dimly lit cavern.

Of course there were no windows, and its only illumination came from a bare light bulb at the far end of the chamber. There, before them, stood another ornate circus wagon. This one differed from the others both in size and in the way it had been maintained. Its gilt scrollwork and painted sides were as fresh as if the work had been done only days before.

As she stared at it, Judy could scarcely choke back tears of rage and terror. She was too frightened to look at him when he spoke.

The voice was quiet, almost soothing, probably the way he spoke to his animals, she thought, the ones who might at any moment turn, pounce upon him, and tear his throat out. But once again, she realized the animals here in captivity were human beings, or whatever remained of their once-human spirit.

"You are my Felidia," he told her, as though caressing her with the words. "I have searched for you all my life. You are the perfect specimen, and at last, here you are."

He was, of course, completely and utterly insane. She knew she must not show her fear.

He led her to a short flight of wooden steps propped beside the cage. He pulled back the gate in the bars and gave another tug on the chain attached to the collar on her neck. She had no choice but to mount the steps and enter the cage.

"You must understand, you will not be harmed," he informed her. "But you must also understand that your life depends on your willingness to be trained. You will have food, water, exercise. But you will also be obedient."

She stared out at him from behind the bars. The insanity reflected in his cold blue eyes was unmistakable and she was overcome with a sense of despair and desperation.

He pointed to the high-topped shoes she always wore when she rode her bike and she knew she was expected to remove them. "I will not tolerate any kind of disobedience," he went on. "Recalcitrant animals must pay the consequences."

She watched him pace agitatedly back and forth in front of the cage, pointing first to one article of her clothing, then another. She had removed the shoes, then the thick cotton socks, then her blouse and the khaki shorts. All that remained were the French-cut underpants she'd pulled on less than twenty-four hours earlier while planning how to convince Horst Von Ziegler to include her in his new circus act.

Could she have been so perilously naive only a day ago? Ellen had tried to warn her, but she'd refused to believe there was any danger spending a couple of hours with a man whose family had once been famous circus performers.

Horst Von Ziegler was the key to her escape. Escape from the suffocation of a small town where everyone knew everyone else. Where everyone did the same predictable thing day after day, year after year. That wasn't the life Judy McAuliffe had promised herself.

When she was in the fifth grade, her mother had taken her to the circus. She'd pleaded for years and finally her mother had agreed. It wasn't something that interested Judy's mother, and there wasn't a lot of spare cash in the household budget for frivolous events, but on Judy's tenth birthday, her mother announced they were going to the circus.

As far as she was concerned, it was the most exciting moment in her life. The swirling spotlights, the deafening brass band, the flying acrobats, but most of all it was the center ring, suddenly filled with animals she'd only seen on television or in books. There they were, posing and leaping and jumping at the flick of a whip. Judy felt her heart pounding in her chest. How she envied all of them. What excitement, day after day. No one she knew had a life like this.

She had dared to dream. Was there anything wrong with that?

She was naked now and felt his eyes staring hungrily back at her from the semidark beyond the cage.

Goosebumps formed on her flesh. She turned away.

"You will not speak," he informed her. "It is a distraction. Henceforth, you will answer to the name 'Felidia.' You are my prized possession. This is a distinction not to be taken lightly. You will be the main attraction of the center ring."

Horst vanished into the darkness, then reappeared seconds later. At first, it wasn't possible to determine what he'd pushed through the bars of her cage. "Dress!" he commanded.

On the floor of the cage was a pair of furry bikini panties with a long tail attached at the rear. Next to it was a halter of the same material, the tawny color that matched the skin of a lion. She tugged the bikini pants up over her buttocks and pulled on the halter as fast as she could. Those eyes devouring her naked body had filled her with a kind of terror she had never experienced.

Fourteen

The dining room was empty when Jim Sweeney came through the door. Ellen was seated by herself, staring through the window, watching cars pass on the road beyond the parking lot. Her heart leapt in her chest when she saw the police cruiser pull into the drive.

"Sorry," he apologized, as he removed his cap and pulled the chair opposite Ellen away from the table. He was feeling a little annoyed that people assumed his time was his own and he could drop everything the moment somebody called. That was the trouble with being a small-town cop. Everyone in town thought they owned you. Even the nice ones like Ellen Wallace.

"Any word?" she asked anxiously.

"Sorry," he said again.

"What am I supposed to do?" she asked. "I can't stand not knowing anything."

Jim was sympathetic but not much help. "You

could file a Missing Person, but to tell you the truth, it's a little soon."

"Meanwhile, I sit and wait. Is that your answer?"

"Judy couldn't wait to get out of this town. We both know that."

"Without her savings and without any clothes?"

"Any strangers in the bar in the last few days?"

"What bar doesn't have strangers? Bud Mosher and I talked about that last night. It's no secret he's had a major case of the hots for Judy for a long time, so he's in here almost every night."

"And?"

"He keeps a jaundiced eye on the proceedings. He didn't see anyone to get excited about. Other than Judy, of course."

"You don't think there's any connection between this and the disappearance of Kathy Kraus, do you?"

"Absolutely not!" Ellen was beginning to feel extremely irritated. She also realized she was beginning to react like Trudy Kraus. What was the matter with the cops around here? Or had the words "foul play" been deleted from the police manual?

"If she had an accident, we'd know it by now."

"I think you should talk to Hans Von Ziegler."

Jim Sweeney stared back intently. It wasn't something he expected her to say, but on some inner gut level, he followed her reasoning. He remembered that morning at the station when Judy inquired about Von Ziegler. They were interrupted when the call came in about the drowning at Stony Creek. In fact, he hadn't given it another thought until this very moment.

"Did she go over to that place?"

"Yes."

"What happened?"

"She met the man. You won't believe it, but she felt sorry for him. She told me he was painfully shy."

"Is that all?"

"Apparently he has a brother who was part of the old circus act. It was the brother Judy really wanted to meet."

"And where is he these days?"

"She knew I wasn't at all happy about this. I tried not to meddle, but I asked her to promise she wouldn't try to go back there."

"Right," he nodded, knowing full well that if Judy McAuliffe intended to go back to the Von Ziegler estate, promises to her aunt weren't likely to keep her away. A door banged behind him and Ellen looked up expectantly.

It was Bud Mosher. A frightened look crossed his face when he saw Ellen deep in conversation with Jim Sweeney.

"Bud!" she called, beckoning him to join them.

He was too anxious to sit down. Leaning against a table, he listened while Ellen gave him a quick rundown on the absence of any information concerning Judy's whereabouts. Finally she announced, "I think she went to the Von Ziegler place."

"Based on what?" he demanded.

"She was there a couple of days ago, Bud. They're a circus family. You know that crazy notion she has about going to Florida this winter. I think she hoped Von Ziegler might have some contacts she could use when she got there."

"Shit!"

"My sentiments exactly."

Jim Sweeney didn't bother to add his own. He was too busy formulating a plan.

"For God's sake, can't you people do something?" Ellen demanded.

"I guess 'you people' means us police, right?"

"Is there anybody else?"

"Me!" Bud erupted. His tall frame hovered ominously over them, as he stared back and forth, from Ellen to Sweeney and back again.

There was a long silence before Jim Sweeney tipped back in his chair. "Mosher, I've got an idea. I could lose my badge for even thinking this, but if I'm right, I could beat out my brother for the next promotion in the family."

When Horst left the cavernous cellar of the great stone mansion, he did not return.

At each new sound, Judy was instantly alert. It was cold and damp. What frightened her more than anything was the fact that the cries and screams she heard were so easily confused with those of jungle beasts. What had he done to these young women to deprive them of their humanity?

She began to consider her own fate and shivered at the thought of it. No matter what happened, she had to remain calm. If she lost her cool, it could mean the end of her.

Furthermore, if and when an opportunity for escape presented itself, it had to work the first time, because she'd never get another. She had to be smarter than he was. Horst Von Ziegler was mad, but he wasn't stupid.

She was unsure how much time had passed when

she heard the shuffling sound of footsteps somewhere in the dim recess of the passage leading to the room where her caged wagon had been stored. She listened, harder this time.

The shuffling sound had stopped.

It was hard to see anything. She peered through the bars and thought she could make out a silhouette standing in the shadows. Her chest tightened, gripped with fear.

The figure did not move. He was watching her. She was certain of it now. The figure began to move.

As it approached and stepped into the light, she almost shouted with relief.

It was Hans.

He stumbled toward the cage and she saw that his eyes were swollen and rimmed with red. He looked furtively over his shoulder, then slipped a bowl of stewed meat between the bars of the cage.

"I should have warned you," he whispered. "I was afraid of this."

"Why didn't you?" she hissed back.

"He would have been furious. I was afraid he would punish us both."

"What do you call this?" she demanded.

"He is obsessed with the new circus act," Hans went on. "You will be his featured lioness, the centerpiece of the new act."

"And the others? They're part of it, too?"

"I wish things could have been different."

"Hans, you have to help me. I've got to get out of here!"

"It's already too late."

"For what?"

"Preparations have been made."

"This is total lunacy! I won't let him do it!"

Hans looked genuinely terrified "You must obey him," he whispered. "He has a ferocious temper. You must not make him angry, I beg of you. You saw what happened to that poor girl hanging from the ceiling."

She'd almost forgotten about Kathy Kraus. Only a short time ago, Judy had been rushing headlong for the highway, determined to contact the police and rescue them all. Now she was a captive herself. Thoughts of Ellen came flooding into her mind. She must be crazed with worry, Judy thought, while she herself was half-crazed with fear.

"If you don't help me, God knows what will happen to us all," she warned.

"No harm will come, if you obey his orders."

"And wind up like those other poor creatures, half out of their minds?" she demanded. "I'd rather die first."

"Please. Don't."

"Then help me. I'm begging you."

"Do as he commands. Please, Felidia. The least little thing can set him off."

"I'm not 'Felidia'! My name is Judy. Don't call me that." This frightening charade had taken on a life of its own and Judy had begun to feel completely powerless to change the course of events.

It was becoming more and more apparent that Hans was as mad as his brother. Gentler but equally mad. No matter what she said, it was impossible to reach him.

"He has forbidden me to speak with you. I must go before he discovers I've disobeyed him."

Which was worse? Trying to reason with another madman or being left alone to wonder what the other one was up to?

"Stay with me just a little longer," she urged, praying that some unexpected brainstorm might turn the tide.

"I will try to come again tomorrow," he said, as he was swallowed up into the shadows at the far end of the chamber.

She sat in the bottom of the cage staring into the bowl Hans had left behind. She raised it to her nose and sniffed at it. She had eaten nothing since breakfast at the Rathskeller the day before. With no spoon or fork to use, Judy was forced to plunge her fingers into the semiliquid contents of the bowl. It was some kind of beef stew, she decided. Its taste wasn't bad and she began to devour it voraciously. Her hands and forearms were stained with juice from the red meat. So were her mouth and cheeks. It slowly dawned on her that the easiest way to get food in her mouth was to kneel on all fours and slurp from the bowl like an animal.

Clearly, that was what he wanted. To tame her into mindless, obedient submission, like one of his beasts from the circus. If that was his intention, Judy vowed, Horst would have his work cut out for him. First, he'd have to destroy her will. She was determined never to let that happen. He might *think* he had succeeded, but Judy would never willingly surrender.

In a moment of utter frustration, she sprang at the bars of her cage, shaking them with all her might. An instant later, she stood perfectly still, realizing she had just played into his hand. First, he would rob her of

137

her precious strength. This was all part of his insane scheme.

She had to be smarter than he was. She must never let down her guard. This was war and she was ready to fight him to the death.

For the time being, she would appear to go along with whatever he wanted. She would gain his confidence and sooner or later Horst would relax his vigilance. When he did, Judy must be ready to make her move.

When Hans returned to his room upstairs, things were in complete disarray. It wasn't the way he'd left it. Shadows crawled back and forth on the wall.

"What took you so long?" the voice asked.

"I brought her food."

"What else?"

"Nothing."

"Liar!"

"I swear."

"What am I to do with you, Hans? I try to be patient, but you continue to disobey me."

"I brought her food. Nothing more."

"You conspired with her to help her escape."

These were the words Hans feared most. How many times had he secretly planned to free the others and how many times had Horst suspected his intent before he could act? The punishments had been brutal. For all their sakes, he must not let this happen again.

In his own peculiar way, he loved that girl down in the cage. If Horst were to banish him, who would be left to protect her?

* * *

In the bottom of her cage, Judy sat licking the inside of the bowl. The food had helped. She realized she had been getting light-headed from hunger. She needed her wits about her now more than ever in her life. She clung to the hope that by this time people would be looking for her, but would they have any idea where to look?

The crypt was deathly quiet.

The other creatures must be sleeping, she thought. It was unlikely that Hans would return, but her mind was racing. Somehow she had to escape, but when? And under what circumstances? If Horst meant to make her a part of his circus act, she'd have to be taken from the cage, but who would do this, Horst or Hans? The harder she thought, the more tired she became. The drowsiness was overpowering, and she began to think she had been drugged. Then she heard the horrifying scream from somewhere above.

It came again. A horrendous shriek of someone in excruciating pain. Again and again shrieks pierced the darkness that surrounded her. She strained to determine where it came from.

There was a deafening ringing in her ears and she felt her consciousness slipping away. Try as she might, she couldn't muster sufficient strength to fight back. No doubt about it, she was sliding into unconsciousness and there wasn't a thing she could do to prevent it.

Horst had won again.

Fifteen

So far, no one had discovered that one of the phone company trucks was missing. If anyone noticed Jim Sweeney rolling out the gate, it didn't seem to be worthy of mention. He was parked at a predetermined spot by the side of a road not far from Stony Creek.

When Bud pulled up in his pickup, Sweeney was checking out telephone equipment. He looked up and grinned as Bud approached.

"Looks like all those summers I spent working with the phone company are starting to pay off." He tossed a leather belt to Bud, then a company hard hat, and tried one on himself. "Convincing?" he asked, then strolled back and forth in front of the truck like a runway model.

"We'd better be," was Bud's only remark.

Before the hour had passed, the two men had parked the phone company van by the iron gate that defended the Von Ziegler estate from unwanted company. A tall pole that guided phone lines onto the property stood fifty feet away.

If they were discovered at this point in their plan, the two had already concocted a story that they were testing the lines for trouble in the area. If no one interrupted, however, Jim would cut the phone line leading to the house.

"This shouldn't take more than a couple of minutes," Jim announced confidently, then dug his cleats into the pole and climbed swiftly to the top.

Bud watched with admiration as Jim hooked up his safety belt and went to work. He cut the wire, then stapled it to the first cross arm so that from the ground it appeared as though it were still attached. When they returned from their visit to the Von Ziegler mansion, he would re-splice the wire.

In the cluttered room he called his studio, Hans stood disconsolately before his easel. Long ago, he'd begun a painting of a lioness he'd remembered from his youth. She was his father's favorite and he would spend hours leading her about the ring at the end of her long tether, hours after the other cats had been returned to their cages.

He had listened as his father purred encouragement to the large beast, as she leapt gracefully from perch to perch. Now and again, she would pose as if awaiting further sounds of approval. And she would not be disappointed. Ilse, his mother, often joked that if Klaus was unfaithful, she would name his "Felidia" as correspondent in the divorce proceedings.

Felidia!

That was a detail he hadn't remembered. How had it escaped him? "Felidia" was the name of his father's favorite cat. "Felidia" was the name Horst had given to this latest captive. Furthermore, he had insisted that she never be referred to as anything else.

The situation was worse than Hans had feared.

He had been furiously working his brushes as he was overcome by memories he'd spent most of his life trying to erase.

Klaus had had his Felidia.

Horst was determined to have his.

A cry of horror escaped him as he stared at the canvas. He had painted Judy McAuliffe's face into that of his father's beloved lioness.

Suddenly, he stood riveted to the spot. He listened intently. It was the unmistakable sound of an engine, but how could that be? He was certain he had locked the gate with not one but two heavy chains at top and bottom.

Hans began to tremble. If he had been careless again, Horst would exact a fearsome price. He hurried toward the front of the building and peered through the drapes.

Sure enough, a telephone truck was nearing the house.

When it stopped, two repairmen appeared from either side and approached the front door.

When the heavy knocking began, he leapt back as though someone had struck him. The pounding continued.

If he refused to answer, perhaps they'd go away.

For a moment, he thought they were gone until the pounding began again, more ferociously this time, at the entrance to the kitchen.

In a paroxysm of panic Hans began to imagine

them breaking windows and forcing their way into the house without his permission. He must stay calm, he told himself repeatedly. Horst would be angry if he let them in, but what would he say if these two burst in uninvited? Horst would never believe him. He had to act fast.

He opened the door only a crack.

"What is it?" he demanded.

"Mr. Von Ziegler?"

He hesitated a moment before answering. So far, he was still safe. "Yes."

The man on the other side of the door had one of the most cheerful smiles he'd ever seen. That was the trouble staying cooped up in this place the way he did. He never met people. And this one seemed to be nice.

"Trouble on the phone lines up here, Mr. Von Ziegler. Is yours okay?"

He wanted to ask him how he got past an iron gate that was trussed in steel, but he was afraid of the answer. "Fine."

The repairman standing behind the one at the door didn't have a face that was nearly as friendly.

"I hope I'm not catching you at a bad time, sir, but we've had calls from all over the area. There's a bug on the line someplace and I've got to check out all the phones to see where it is." The nice young man was pushing the door open. He was coming in. So was the other one! Horst wouldn't like this at all.

His smile was so open and friendly, Hans didn't know why he was so frightened. Stay calm, the voice inside instructed him. Be firm and get rid of them.

Before he knew what was happening, the smiling

143

repairman had lifted his phone from the hook. He stood, head cocked to one side, listening. "Dead as a mackerel," he announced. "You said it was okay. When did you use it last?"

Get rid of them, the voice said again. It was hard to listen to both at the same time.

"I, ah, I can't remember," he stammered.

The repairmen were all business now. The first had stopped smiling and unscrewed the mouthpiece on the phone. The other was following the telephone wire stapled to the baseboard on the wall. It led to the door to the basement.

"Stop!" Hans shouted, unable to control himself.

The second repairman looked startled; he had one hand on the door latch and was about to lift it. "Gotta trace these wires," he explained.

"I tell you no!" Hans insisted. "You cannot use that door."

The one with the pleasant face screwed the parts of the receiver back together. "This tests out okay. Where's the box where the phone lines enter the house?"

"I'll show you," Hans said. "No need to go down there. Follow me."

Jim and Bud exchanged glances. From the look on Bud's face, Jim knew he wanted to get a look behind that door, but he cocked his head in Hans's direction, indicating that for the time being, at least, they should play along.

Hans led them to a bulkhead door at one end of the house. They followed him down a steep flight of stone steps. At the bottom, it was dark and musty smelling. Bud pulled a flashlight off his tool belt and switched it on. Strands of spiderwebs hung from the ceiling.

They moved along a narrow passage until they reached a heavy wooden door. It creaked ominously when Hans pushed it open.

The air was damp and their footsteps echoed off the walls. Bud moved his flashlight back and forth and saw they were in a cavelike vault. The stone walls were crumbling and dusty.

High overhead was the metallic box that housed the telephone wires. It looked as though no one had come near it in decades.

Jim turned to Bud. "I'm going to need a ladder. Better get the small one out of the truck."

He turned to leave, and as he did, Bud's blood ran cold. Two rats the size of grown cats scurried past him and disappeared into the darkness.

"Jesus Christ!" he yelled. His voice echoed down the passageway.

"We don't use this wing under normal circumstances," Hans explained, with an unmistakable note of apology in his voice. "I'd be most appreciative if you'd finish your business as quickly as possible. I'm expecting someone."

When Bud returned with the ladder, Jim propped it up under the phone box and climbed so that he was at eye level with the wires. He pulled a screwdriver from his belt and began to work the connecting screws inside. Again, he pulled the receiving device from the hook on his belt and held it to his ear.

"There's some weird interference on this line, sir," he announced finally. "How many phones you got here?"

"One," Hans lied.

"Doesn't seem that way." He replaced the screws inside the box and hung the receiver back on his belt, then retraced his steps down the ladder.

"Sorry for the inconvenience, sir," he said, mopping his forehead under the hardhat. "We're gonna keep looking, but if we don't find the trouble, we may be back."

Hans was relieved at the very notion they might be leaving. It helped him keep calm, knowing he wouldn't have to keep making up answers each time they asked a question.

"My pleasure," he decided to say, when it was at the back of his mind to tell them he'd rather die than open the door to them again. As it was, Horst was going to be very angry.

He watched through the crack in the drapes as they got back in the telephone van, started the engine, and disappeared down the drive.

When they were gone, he knew that Horst was watching. Of course, he'd seen everything. There was no point trying to deny it. That would only make things worse, and they were bad enough already.

Hans began to tremble. He wet his lips and tried to control the convulsive shaking that racked his slender frame.

"You have done it again," Horst jeered at him accusingly. "Strangers! Two of them!"

"I couldn't help it," he tried to apologize, but it fell on deaf ears.

"I have warned you again and again and still you disobey me!"

"It wasn't my fault," he whined.

146

"Was it *mine?*" Horst roared back at him.

His face gleaming with perspiration, Hans took several nervous little steps, then stood cowering in a corner.

"Bad boy. Bad, bad boy," Horst taunted him. "Come and get your punishment."

"Not again," Hans pleaded, his eyes riveted on the string of rawhide Horst was extracting from his pocket.

"Take down your pants!" he commanded. "Bad boys must be punished."

Sobbing uncontrollably, Hans slowly removed his pants and dropped them to his ankles.

"Off!" Horst commanded again.

This time, Hans slipped off his underwear, and when he did, Horst wrapped the rawhide around his shriveled testicles, yanking it hard.

He screeched in pain. As if on cue, Horst applied more pressure until the swollen, purple-veined scrotum looked as if it would explode.

The two were silent for a long while as they drove back to the half-deserted road where Bud had left his pickup. During the ride, Bud glanced out the window and realized the sun would be going down soon.

"What's next?" he asked finally.

"I'm not sure," Jim replied, staring noncommittally at the road in front of him.

"There's something weird going on at that place. I say we go back."

"Look, I could get my ass reamed for what we've done already."

Bud stared at him for a long moment. "Did that

147

blue uniform turn you into some kind of pussy, or what? A few years ago, getting your ass reamed never entered your mind." Bud struck a nerve and he knew it.

"Goddammit, I need a warrant!"

"The fuck you do. I say we go back."

Jim Sweeney was torn between his old lust for adventure and everything he'd learned about solid police procedure. If Bud Mosher's instincts were correct, he had to make a clean arrest. Too many criminals walked the streets because of cops who didn't get it right the first time around. "I'm thinking," he said finally.

"Well, don't make a career of it," Bud snapped and then fell silent. A plan was taking shape at the back of his mind. He decided not to tell Jim Sweeney about the window he'd unlocked before they left the mansion.

Jim Sweeney had returned the van to the phone company parking lot and picked up his cruiser when suddenly its radio came alive with a blast of static.

"Sweeney? This is Desk Sergeant O'Hara. Do you copy?"

He took the transmitter from the dashboard. "Loud and clear. Over."

Another burst of static followed. "They've found a motorcycle in the creek about a half a mile past the Ackerman farm."

"I'm on my way. Over and out." He spun the cruiser around, hit the siren, and floored the accelerator. He could overtake Bud Mosher heading back to

Ruttenburg, provided he didn't encounter any unexpected obstructions along the way.

He caught up with him just as Bud was making the turn onto Route 32.

"That siren of yours scared the shit out of me," Bud told him as he leaned through the driver's window of the pickup. "What the hell do you want?"

"They've found a motorcycle at the bottom of Stony Creek. Follow me. But don't tell anybody I invited you."

The cruiser sped off with Bud's small truck right behind. When they neared the spot where the bike had been found, another cruiser sat parked, its blinking red light indicating that this was the place. Both vehicles pulled off the road and onto the grass.

Sweeney and Mosher hurried to the bank of the creek. About twenty feet below, several policemen and a group of kids made a tight circle around the corpse of a battered motorcycle.

They scurried down the embankment, slipping and sliding until they reached the bottom.

Bud paled once they were able to take a closer look. When Jim glanced at him for confirmation that the bike was indeed Judy's, Bud didn't say a word. He closed his eyes and nodded sadly.

The fenders were badly dented and it was dripping with water. Weeds that grew at the bottom of the creek had wound themselves through the spokes of the wheels and around the handlebars.

"These dents didn't come from a collision," Jim whispered to Bud. "It looks like someone took a hammer to the bike, then dumped it in the creek."

Bud ran his hand along the seat as though he were

caressing it, while a gut-wrenching combination of anger and fear began to assert itself in the pit of his stomach. Somewhere behind him he heard the police talking among themselves.

"The Helmer boys were fishing out in the middle of the creek when they spotted something shiny. Jeff, here, the oldest one, dove in to get a look. He's the one who got a rope around the handlebars and he and his four buddies dragged it in."

Bud didn't hear everything they said, but he did pick up on the fact that a police launch was on its way. They intended to drag the area in search of a body. He stared helplessly toward the center of the greenish brown water.

One winter a few years earlier, he'd helped a crew of rescue workers drag Williams Lake for a kid who had fallen through the ice. He remembered what the boy had looked like when they finally hauled him out. His lips were purple and the flesh turned blue the moment it hit the air.

Bud wasn't sure what he'd do if they found Judy down there. The one thing he knew was that he had to stay and wait, no matter what.

Within minutes came the sputter of a distant motor. The sputter became a roar and the launch came around the bend of the creek. Bud's heart sank at the sight of four men in the stern, dressed in wet suits. Clearly, they expected the worst.

The sun had gone down and the light was beginning to fade. The police launch had crisscrossed a wide body of water surrounding the spot where the motorcycle had been found.

Sweeney had talked his way onto the rescue launch, but meanwhile Bud sat on the bank of the creek, watching helplessly.

His heart stopped when he heard the motor cut and begin to idle. A voice reached him across the water. "I've got something!"

Bud could see one of the wet suits working a long pole at the stern of the launch. He closed his eyes, then opened them again. When he did, he saw three wet suits surrounding the first. The bow of the launch was pointing in Bud's direction, blocking his view, but from the way the four men peered into the waters below them, he knew they were trying to bring something up. One of them jumped over the side of the boat.

"Oh, God," he found himself praying aloud. "Please, no." Tears stung his eyes. He jumped to his feet and ran to the edge of the water.

The man in the water was struggling to bring something to the surface. Water splashed all around him.

Then came a cheer from the back of the boat as a traffic stop sign was hauled on board.

Bud felt weak in the knees as he watched the police launch head toward shore.

When Jim Sweeney stood beside him once again, his voice sounded miles away. "I don't think she's down there. But they'll be back tomorrow when they've got more light. Just in case. Let's go."

They turned and retraced their footsteps up the bank of the creek.

Sixteen

She awoke with a start. For a fleeting moment, before reality closed in, Judy didn't know where she was.

Then the musty odor of mildew assailed her nostrils, and as her eyes adjusted to the gloom, she could make out the bars of her cage. It was cold and drafty. All she wore was a skimpy halter and a pair of panties made from some kind of fake fur.

Horst had taken her watch along with everything else. She had no idea what time it was.

The quiet of the dungeonlike basement was disrupted occasionally by far-off shrieks from his other captives.

Her arms and legs were stiff and sore. She wasn't sure which had done more damage, the repeated falls back into that animal trap in the woods the night before or sleeping on the hard floor of the cage that now held her prisoner.

A door opened and closed. She heard footsteps

making their way in her direction. It was dark and she could see almost nothing, yet she stared apprehensively through the bars into the obscurity beyond.

If it was Horst . . . She trembled at the thought of what was sure to happen next.

As the figure approached, she had her answer even before she saw the face. The stooped shoulders, the tentative steps, told her it was Hans.

He was carrying a heavy ring of keys.

Judy's heart leapt with expectation. Was it possible he had dared defy his brother and would help her to escape?

She began to speak, but Hans held a finger to his lips. Scarcely daring to breath, she watched as he inserted a shiny brass key into the padlock that secured the cage.

With an unmistakable tenderness, Hans held her hand as she jumped from the cage to the stone floor below. She longed to throw her arms about his neck in gratitude, but something told her she must not. At least, not yet.

"You won't be sorry," she said, forming the words into a scarcely audible whisper.

Again, he held his finger to his lips. It was a signal that neither of them must speak.

Without a sound, he reached into his pocket, withdrew a chain, and attached it to the steel collar that encircled her neck.

"What are you doing?" she screamed at him, her hopes for imminent freedom dashed like the snuffing of a candle.

His reply was to spin her about, take her by the shoulders, and shake her furiously. From the wild and terrified look in his eyes, Judy was certain Horst was lurking somewhere close-by. He tugged on the chain, and led her up a flight of slippery stone steps and out of the basement.

Judy realized they were somewhere on the main floor of the house when she found herself at the foot of what must have once been an elaborate, sweeping staircase. Hans ran halfway up, then turned, giving the chain a sharp pull, indicating that she was to follow. They climbed the stairs and at the top they entered an oak-paneled foyer with a crystal chandelier hanging from its carved ceiling, now covered with a lacy canopy of dust and cobwebs as delicate as the bits of sculpted glass that formed its massive structure.

Off to one side was another ornately carved and brightly painted circus wagon, its metal gate hanging open and waiting. Judy looked furtively about. Was it possible to dash for it and get down the stairs before Hans could stop her? He still had a tight grip on the chain and snapped it once again, letting her know with a single flick of the wrist that any thought she might have of escaping would be to court disaster, perhaps for both of them.

He jerked his head toward the circus wagon. Judy knew this was her signal to get inside it. She had to remind herself that her only hope for escape was to pretend to be docile and obedient. Otherwise, how could she lull either one of them into the mistaken belief that she had been properly subdued?

Refusing any assistance from Hans, Judy hoisted herself onto the floor of the wagon, swung her feet inside, and crawled in.

Its gate slammed shut and once more came the familiar metallic click reminding her she was a prisoner of these two madmen.

Without warning, Hans pulled a ripcord and heavy drapes dropped on all sides of the cage, plunging her into an airless darkness.

She wasn't sure how long she sat there, wondering what new degradation was sure to follow. Time passed and the wait seemed endless. It was so stuffy behind the heavy drapes, she found it hard to breathe. Each time she sucked air into her lungs, she became more light-headed. It was a fight to remain conscious.

She was afraid she'd started to hallucinate when the first faint whines of calliope music began to sound in her ears. There then followed a sometimes-discordant blare of trumpets, cornets, trombones, and drums. They made a couple of false starts, but there it was again. Somewhere, a circus band was blasting away at full volume. Despite the deadening effect of the drapes that enveloped her cage, its sound was almost painful.

The wagon began to roll until finally the din of brassy music seemed to surround her completely.

Where was she? And what was happening?

The answer came when the drapes were raised with the same swift motion by which they'd been dropped.

Horst stood off to one side, a bullwhip in one hand, a brass key in the other. He was wearing the brilliant red coat with shiny brass buttons and gold braid he seemed to favor, but also a tall black hat that glistened in the spotlight where he stood. He made a low and formal bow to the tiers of empty bleachers lining the walls.

The cage where Judy sat had been positioned on

one side of a vast room which must have once served as a formal ballroom for the Von Ziegler mansion. Directly opposite was another cage of much larger proportions and held more of Horst's "cats," all clad in halters and panties similar to the ones Judy had been given soon after her capture.

Otherwise, there was no one else in the room. Where was Hans? she wondered. Where was that music coming from? Seconds later she realized that the circus music emanated from concert-sized speakers mounted on the walls at all four corners of the room.

A passageway about three feet wide and three feet high, enclosed in wire mesh, was attached to the entrance of the cage on the far side of the room. It led to an opening in the caged area at the middle of the room that created Horst's "center ring."

Suddenly, the music stopped. Horst cracked his whip.

"Now, Shebas!" he screamed, his voice ricocheting off the walls and ceiling of the spacious, vaulted room.

The passage from cage to the center ring forced his captives to crawl on hands and knees to get from one place to the other. When the cage was finally emptied and the wire tunnel was filled with crawling "cats," he pulled a lever and opened a gate to the center ring.

With a dramatic sweep of his arm, the bullwhip unfurled. As each of them crawled through the passage and into the ring, he delivered a menacing crack above each of their heads. There was no need to do it twice. These were "cats" he had painstakingly trained. They knew the consequence of even the slightest deviance from the performance he demanded. All of them wore huge, ugly welts across their backs.

Von Ziegler's eyes gleamed with a wild rage and his face glistened with sweat. He cracked the whip again and again. The veins on his neck bulged like thick blue ropes as he shouted his commands.

Judy watched in utter disbelief as one after the other leapt to a perch or platform like driven beasts. With each new crack of Horst's whip, they would assume a pose, hopping from platform to platform until each of them was back where she started, trembling with exhaustion and fear. Some would growl and paw at the bullwhip when Horst mockingly dangled it before them.

He shouted orders, cracked the whip, and drove them to perform stunt after stunt. When at last he seemed satisfied, they squatted back on their haunches, breathing heavily and gleaming with sweat.

For a brief moment, Horst cast the bullwhip aside and raised a wide hoop in the air. He held it an arm's length in front of him, then reached into the pocket of his white jodhpurs and produced a silver lighter. With a flick of its wheel, it burst into flame. Horst held it to the hoop and smiled triumphantly as its entire circumference was set ablaze.

Again, he reached for the whip, gave it a double crack this time, and strode majestically toward the lineup of his obedient "cats."

Flames danced in their eyes. The first sprang from her perch, dove through the hoop, and made a perfect somersault into a bed of straw piled on the other side at the spot where she would land. The second did the same. And the third. And the fourth.

None dared to hesitate.

Failure to perform with absolute precision meant punishment far more hideous than being scorched by flames.

One after another, they dove through the burning hoop. By the time they had completed a third rotation, Judy saw how the strenuous performance had taken its toll. Each of their movements had turned slow and deliberate. Once the dive through the hoop was complete, several of them lost their balance, on the far side, falling with a painful thud onto their chins.

Finally, one of them miscalculated completely. As she dove, she crashed into the hoop, knocked it from Horst's hands, and it fell on her back. She screamed in pain as the fire seared her skin and ignited the straw on which she lay. Her hair exploded in flames.

Furious, Horst lunged for the buckets of water he kept close-by. One after the other, he dumped them on her, until the flames were finally extinguished. With no regard for what had just occurred, he yanked her to her feet, then smacked her buttocks and the backs of her legs with the handle of his whip.

She howled in pain, but slowly and obediently returned to her perch.

Frozen with fear, Judy watched as Horst approached her cage. During the entire time his "cats" had performed, she heard nothing from them that even remotely resembled human sound. Shrill animal cries had come from expressionless creatures with eyes that were dull and lifeless.

Suddenly, and without warning, the circus music began to blare once again. Horst marched in time to its brassy cadence. With elaborate ceremony, he unlocked the entrance to Judy's cage and reached for the handle of the chain attached to the collar fastened around her neck.

He gave it a nasty pull, telling her she'd be very wise to do whatever he demanded.

Cautiously, she descended the wooden steps placed beneath the entrance to the cage.

Horst cracked his whip and led her to the perimeter of the ring, then he returned and stood at its center. Again and again, he cracked the whip, forcing her to prance about the rim of the ring with the wide, loping stride of a prowling jungle cat.

Moments later, he dropped the chain and turned his back. When he faced her once again, she saw he was holding a three-legged stool, its stubby feet pointing directly at her. What did he want her to do? she wondered. Then came the sudden realization that this mad charade had taken on a new dimension.

He wanted her to become a ferocious and menacing jungle beast. She must lunge at him again and again until he tamed her into docile submission. It was an exercise in lunatic fantasy and she had no recourse but to comply. It would have even been funny if Horst were not so deadly serious.

In desperation, Judy's eyes roamed the room for a reassuring glimpse of Hans somewhere in the darkness beyond.

Brash, raucous music pounded in her ears. Each time she lunged in Horst's direction, he flicked his bullwhip closer and closer to her face. Sweat ran off her forehead and into her eyes.

She reeled about dizzily, then felt the excruciating

sting of the whip that splashed across the naked skin of her back. For a moment, she thought she was going to vomit. She gagged and retched, momentarily oblivious to the person insisting on this torturous exercise.

Judy staggered about in the suffocating heat of the lights, searching for a cooler spot where she could breathe more easily.

Her back was burning where the lash of Horst's whip had broken the skin, but what she really needed was air.

She felt his stare as she paced back and forth, desperate for relief from this suffocating heat. Her hair hung in damp loose strands around her face. It covered her eyes and her head began to spin. Finally, a merciful darkness closed in as she collapsed in a heap at the center of the ring.

Horst Von Ziegler thrust his arms above his head in a gesture of triumph and victory, savoring the thrill of incontestable domination. Like his father before him, he had tamed his Felidia. He had earned his place as Master of the Ring.

First to one side and then to the other Horst bowed majestically, acknowledging the applause that resounded in his head.

Slowly, he proceeded to the spot where Judy lay crumpled on the floor. She was still unconscious as he raised her in his arms and held her before him like a sacrifice to some unseen gods.

With that, he strode from the room, her limp body dangling from his arms.

Seventeen

The only illumination she could perceive came from someplace far away. She shivered with cold and realized she was now completely naked, lying on a hard, damp surface. It was definitely not the floor of her cage.

What had he done with her? The wound on her back still burned. She felt drained of all strength and almost unable to move. If an opportunity for escape presented itself, could she even attempt it?

Little by little, her eyes adjusted to a new kind of darkness. She was inside a cell hewn from the craggy rock of the mansion's foundation. If only she had the strength to get up and move about, she was sure she'd discover it must be at least three times the size of the cage where she'd been held captive. Maybe in the morning when Hans brought her food she would be able to see it better.

She had almost fallen asleep when she thought she heard a noise. The floor was cold and damp, but she lay without moving, listening for some sound to inform her what new and diabolical twist Horst's mind may have taken. It came again.

She held her breath, trying not to make even the slightest sound. It was perilously close. Perhaps inside the cell!

For a long while, she heard nothing more. Still, the cold hand of fear gripped her heart.

An inky blackness obscured the place where she was now imprisoned. She could make out only the dimmest of shadows, yet she knew something or someone was there. She felt the air stir and smelled the musky odor of another living creature.

Suddenly, the terrifying thought crossed her mind. Was it possible Horst had wild beasts imprisoned beneath the house as well? She felt a surge of adrenaline as new questions formed at the back of her mind. Was he putting her to a test of sheer physical survival? Or was it something else, far worse?

This time the sound was unmistakable. A low, guttural, growling sound came from the darkness, then a scraping noise as something moved toward her.

It pounced and landed its full weight upon her, forcing the air from her lungs. It was the first sound she'd made. Judy screamed and fought the beast off as best she could, but its brute animal strength was too powerful. It sprawled on top of her. Its coarse and bristly coat stung like needles pricking her naked flesh. Sharp teeth sank into her throat. Judy jerked her face away to escape the suffocating stench of its rank, foul breath.

A hardness poked at her belly.

My God, she realized, filled with a sickening horror and desperation. This drooling beast is going to rape me!

She felt her legs pried apart and screamed in pain as

its member drove deep inside her. She screamed again and again. It was on her still, rutting and growling in bestial fury.

Judy felt she was being ripped apart when suddenly the beast reared its head with a full-throated and torturous roar. Seconds later, it collapsed with a whimper and fell.

Once she dared risking the slightest move, she gave it a disgusted shove. It rolled off onto its back beside her.

After what had just happened, she wasn't sure she cared anymore if she escaped or not. She stared at the impenetrable darkness surrounding her, riveted to the spot where she lay. Tears were too trivial to express how hopeless she felt.

A mind-numbing daze encompassed her brain. She no longer heard or felt anything.

A short while later, when Horst gathered up the mangy skin of lion's fur he'd been wearing and slipped away into the dark, Judy was too dazed to notice.

At the edge of the woods, not more than fifty yards from the Von Ziegler mansion, Bud Mosher crouched behind a sprawling and overgrown hedge.

He had been watching the house for hours.

Occasionally, he had been able to detect a faint glimmer of lights burning behind the heavy drapes that shrouded the windows, but for quite some time the place was in complete darkness.

Once he was certain that all activity inside had concluded for the day, he would make a dash for it and hope that the window he'd unlocked on his previous visit had not been discovered.

It had been hot and humid all day, the temperature in the mid-nineties, but once the sun set, a breeze sprang up off the river and it was cooler now, with even the faintest hint of autumn in the air. Bud decided it was time to make a dash for it. He moved swiftly from behind the hedge, across part of the sloping lawn, and into the deeper shadows of the house itself. Flat up against the stone wall, he paused and listened. He heard only the sounds of a late summer night, not even the distant barking of a dog.

Stealthily, he made his way around the building, careful to remain as close to the wall as he possibly could. In the dark, it was hard to know exactly which window was the one he'd unlatched. It was close-by the kitchen, but in the dark, they all looked the same.

He tried several, all steadfastly unyielding, until one of them quite unexpectedly slid silently upward. Bud held his breath.

He raised the window inches at a time. The silence inside the great mansion was almost painful to his ears as he strained for some indication as to where its occupants might be. Sound asleep, he prayed. He would have to find his way with tedious caution, making certain that floors did not creak, that furniture in his path did not suddenly and noisily move, alerting the occupants of the house to the presence of an intruder below.

He had a small pocket flashlight with him, but he only planned to use it in short bursts to illuminate a course he would then follow in complete darkness.

He hadn't told Jim Sweeney about the unlocked window. Bud began to wonder if maybe that was a mistake. If he, too, disappeared mysteriously from town, what would people ask themselves? Someone was sure to say that he and Judy had planned the whole thing. They had eloped, it was as simple as that.

Everything in Ruttenburg was supposed to have a simple answer. No one expected anything else.

Without warning, Bud caught a sudden glimpse of movement from the corner of his eye. He whirled about.

On the far side of the room he could just barely see the outline of a man in a shaft of moonlight that entered the room through parted drapes. He stepped back into the shadows and the man disappeared as well. There was no sound except that of his own heavy breathing. If this person had slipped into hiding somewhere nearby, where had he gone?

Bud felt sure that if it got down to a contest of one-on-one physical strength, he would emerge victorious. The realization bolstered his courage and urged him to move in the direction where the other had stood. He slid noiselessly along the edge of the room until another flash of movement spun him about.

In the faint light of the room, he discovered himself face to face with his own image in a floor-to-ceiling mirror.

Somewhere far off, a clock struck twelve.

He was determined to find what lay beyond the door that Von Ziegler had refused to let them open while he and Sweeney had played at being phone men. In fact, it was the precise reason Bud had decided to return alone.

Search warrants were not a necessary part of his plan.

Moments later, Bud found himself in a pantry, just

off the kitchen. Against one wall was a huge restaurant-sized freezer. Strange, he thought, this Von Ziegler guy must have bought enough frozen food to keep him for a year, if he ever filled that thing even once.

What made him cross the room to look inside, Bud wasn't sure. Yet he did it just the same. Its contents made him nearly drop the lid on his own hand. He felt his legs go weak and rubbery.

"Oh, Jesus, God!" he said aloud. He stared at a severed human leg and the upper part of a female torso, breasts and all. His head swam and he had to lean against the freezer to get his strength back. But somewhere in the recess of his mind, he knew that those large and pendulous breasts could not have belonged to Judy McAuliffe.

Now, more than ever, he was convinced she was here somewhere, and he didn't intend to waste another precious moment. That locked door was the answer, he knew it. His mind reeled with the awful reality of what he'd just discovered.

He stumbled around in the darkness, then reminded himself that a vital part of his mission was to perform with catlike quiet. What good would it do to find Judy only to be discovered while trying to escape?

A quick burst of light from his pocket flash showed the way to the door he'd been prevented from opening previously. He wondered if he'd have to pick the lock or remove its hinges, but, much to his surprise, it opened easily the moment he lifted its latch.

The small flashlight gave only meager assistance as he picked his way down a flight of loose and uneven stone steps.

* * *

For the first time in a week, Ellen and Harry had gone to bed without the drone of the air conditioner humming from across the room. A breeze had sprung up during the evening and the temperature had dropped along with the humidity.

Harry could sleep through a tornado, she had always said. Ellen was the light sleeper of the two. The quiet of the room was as disturbing as any noise she could imagine.

It was her imagination that was keeping her awake.

Where was Bud Mosher? When he didn't show up for happy hour, Ellen decided he'd been kept late at the shop with unexpected business. When he didn't appear at dinnertime or join the crowd that usually gathered at the bar just before closing, she started to become frantic with worry.

This was one disappearance too many. And too many to be a coincidence. She thought about poor Trudy again and her heart went out to her.

Never underestimate a mother's intuition, she remembered her own mother saying, with more frequency than she had appreciated at the time. Trudy knew there was something wrong from the very beginning and no one believed her.

Well, an aunt's intuition isn't anything to be sneezed at either, she told herself. Knowing that was of very little comfort. First thing in the morning, she planned to stop off at Bud's shop. If he wasn't there, she would have to convince the police they had plenty of reason to begin a thorough investigation, whether they agreed with her or not.

The stone floor of the basement made quiet movement nearly impossible as Bud moved from one passage to another. Finally, he found himself in a larger, more open area. A quick flash of the light revealed something that looked like a huge wagon parked next to a wall. He shut off the light and moved closer. For a split second, he shone the light once again and discovered that what he saw was a large, ornate circus wagon.

Of course, he told himself, why not? The Von Zieglers were a famous circus family. They must have had lots of old circus equipment around the place years ago. He decided to chance another quick peek around the room. The beam of his light fell on another wagon, next to the one where he was standing, and two more on the far side of the room.

A strange noise from inside the wagon interrupted his thoughts. More rats the size of house pets? He had no weapon, but maybe if he shone the light on them, it might frighten them away.

He pointed the tiny flashlight in the direction the noise had come from and pushed the switch.

To Bud's amazement and utter horror, two half-crazed human eyes stared back at him. The creature lying in the bottom of the cage was no more than a teenager, scarcely past childhood, but the eyes looked like they had witnessed unspeakable horror.

Bud's thoughts flew to Judy. If she was imprisoned like a trapped animal in this subterranean dungeon, he was determined to find her and set her free.

The beam of light fell into one cage and then another. He must have found nine or ten young females lying half-naked on the floor of those cages. Some looked back at him through heavy-lidded eyes; some made no movement at all.

Oh, God, he thought. She's here. I know it.

The cavernous cellar was damp and drafty. A suffocating stench of human waste clung to its walls.

"Judy!" he called in a voice that sounded more like a hoarse stage whisper. "It's Bud. Where are you?"

One of the circus wagons began to creak. He ran in the direction of the noise, but when he played his light through its bars, the naked female trapped inside was no one he had ever seen.

Desperately, he ran from cage to cage, with the frantic hope she might be in one of them. His mind was numb with fear for her safety, and he silently prayed that somewhere in this vast dungeon he would find her still alive.

Each wagon he inspected produced new cries and whimpering from the pitiful beings trapped within. My God, he thought as their sound increased, they'll ruin everything! Speed, stealth, and silence were his only weapons. Without them, his mission could be doomed.

"Judy!" he called again, his whisper echoing like wind through the cavernous dungeon.

His head began to swim with blurred images of the human parts he uncovered in the freezer on the floor above. What made him so certain none of them was Judy's? He didn't know. It was a chance he had to take. Otherwise, how could he live with himself?

Crack!

Bud heard the sharp report, like a rifle shot, seconds before the bullwhip slapped the floor beside his foot. He whirled about. Even in the darkness, he knew he was facing a man slightly smaller than he was.

If size were the only factor, Bud knew he had the upper hand. But it was a bullwhip he'd heard crack.

With stunning swiftness, the whip cracked again, slashing Bud across the forearm, leaving a deep gash of open flesh. Unsuccessfully, he tried to grasp its stinging coil, at the same time cursing himself for coming here alone and weaponless.

The next crack caught him across the eyes, nearly blinding him. He danced from side to side, trying vainly to escape the twisting, thrashing, serpentlike whip. He staggered backward, unseeing, suddenly aware the odds of getting out alive were virtually nonexistent.

For a split second, he saw Jim Sweeney in his mind's eye, hunched over the wheel of the telephone van. He remembered how mad he was that Jim was playing it safe. Maybe the academy put some sense in his head. Sense was something Bud usually had in spades. But this day, his heart urged him on. His brain played no part in this expedition.

Again and again the black serpent lashed out, ripping his scalp and face. The pain was so fierce, he couldn't think, but somewhere, in the recess of his mind, he knew he'd failed her.

The final crack of the snakelike coil encircled his throat. Bud couldn't save either one of them now.

Eighteen

His head was throbbing with a pain more excruciating than any he'd ever known. Why was it always like this? Why did Horst always leave him with the mess he left behind?

A fresh, cool breeze wafting through the tiny crack in his bedroom window made him shiver and reminded him of the exhausting work that lay ahead of him.

Horst was asleep, of course. He always slept when there was work like this to be done. In truth, Hans was almost glad. He didn't have the energy and emotional stamina to confront him again this morning.

Hans would go about his chores without a word. He would say nothing. At least, not for the time being.

Horst thought he had been so clever.

Of course, it would be his ruination, and probably the ruination of both of them, unless Hans could find some way to stop him.

Last night had been the worst of all. Hans had seen everything. Just as he'd seen everything the night that Ilse and Klaus were mauled to death by their father's favorite lioness.

Horst had been waiting for that moment almost all his entire life. How ironic that his father's favorite had ripped their throats out. The prized Felidia who prowled majestically between them at the head of the circus parade.

She was scarcely more than a cub when they returned with her from Africa. After that, Ilse and Klaus Von Ziegler were never photographed without her. Her face was seen on posters and billboards wherever the Circus Von Ziegler had traveled.

What happened that night in the ring was almost inconceivable.

The memory was so ghastly Hans could not erase it from his brain. That was when the headaches had begun, sometimes so blindingly painful he thought his skull would crack in two.

A crumpled workshirt lay on the floor beside him. As though in a trance, he bent over, picked it up, and slipped it on. It hung from his shoulders in loose folds, but he gave it no further thought. There was far too much to be done.

By this time, the cats would be awake. How many had been roused from their slumber the night before when Horst dragged the body of that telephone man through the basement, up the steps, and into the pantry above?

As usual, Horst had left him with the worst of it. The blade that slashed the telephone man's throat had ripped through his windpipe and esophagus, but there was the nasty business of dealing with a head that flopped around like the bud of a broken

172

flower, not completely separated from its stem. Luckily, he kept the blade of his heavy cleaver honed razor-sharp. One deft blow, maybe two, would suffice. It was the limbs that were the problem.

The telephone man was tall. The legs would have to be butchered immediately into smaller pieces. The freezer was already filled to overflowing.

At least the weather was in his favor. The hint of autumn in the fresh morning air meant he could fill the cauldron he used for stewing and get rid of some of it immediately.

Harry was in the shower when Ellen hurried downstairs and out the door. The less said about where she was going, and what she hoped to achieve, the better.

As she sped along the winding country road, she heard her tires screech when she rounded a sharp turn at the entrance to the bridge over Stony Creek. The sun glinted off the surface of the water below. It was a perfect day, but Ellen gave no thought at all to the weather or the view.

She was too busy trying to figure out what to do next. Just as she feared, Bud Mosher's service station was locked tight when she pulled up next to the pumps. The shop was always open at eight o'clock sharp. It was already ten and there was no sign of Bud anywhere. Someone named Vince had stuck a note in Bud's door saying he'd be back later to pick up the car battery Bud ordered for him.

A voice deep within was telling Ellen to go straight to the police station, to find Jim Sweeney and talk to him privately. Something had to be done.

Instead, she found herself speeding toward Rhinelander, trying to figure out what she'd say to this Von Ziegler person when she rang his doorbell. She ran through several scenarios and rejected them all. She could hardly say, "Hello, I'm Ellen Wallace and I believe you know where I can find my niece." Nor could she barge inside and demand to search the house. Being the census taker would have to suffice. The papers were full of the importance of having an accurate count. If someone had been there previously, she'd simply say that they were double-checking the county figures or something. She doubted he'd know the difference anyway.

It was still early. The main street of Rhinelander was almost deserted. Outside a small grocery store with a sign that read Rossler's Market, a paunchy, middle-aged man was smoking a cigarette and sweeping the sidewalk.

Ellen slowed the car, then stopped at the curb when he paused for a moment to relight his cigarette. She leaned her elbow through the open window.

"Are you Mr. Rossler, by any chance?" It was a safe question for starters, and if she was wrong it couldn't do any harm. At least she'd opened the conversation.

The man examined the end of the butt for a long moment, put it back in his mouth, drew on it, then eyed her cautiously through the smoke curling up from the glow on its tip.

"What can I do for you?" he asked noncommittally.

"I understand the Von Ziegler estate is somewhere around here. Could you point me in the right direc-

174

tion?" She hoped the apprehension forming a hard ball at the pit of her stomach hadn't made its way to her face.

The man's eyes narrowed for a moment. He drew on the cigarette again and took it from his mouth.

"Afraid I can't help you, there," he replied finally.

Ellen knew he was fudging. He didn't say he didn't know, only that he couldn't help her. Or wouldn't.

She decided to try again. "The circus family. You must have heard of them. They've got a big estate out here somewhere. I don't think it's far, but I'm not sure which road it's on."

"Me neither," said the man and began to sweep the sidewalk once again. He turned his back and began to move the broom with such ferocity, Ellen thought he'd uproot one of the cement squares if he didn't take it easy.

"Thanks anyway," she called affably as she hit the accelerator and headed up the street.

The Rhinelander post office was set back from the road a short distance from the block of stores that lined Main Street and formed the center of town. Von Ziegler must get mail, Ellen thought. Someone in the post office must know where the place is.

There was a female postal employee behind the counter furiously pounding envelopes with a rubber stamp when Ellen came through the glass doors at the front of the tidy brick building. The years she'd spent dealing with customers at the Rathskeller had taught her to size people up in a couple of seconds, but this woman was so completely expressionless Ellen wasn't sure where to begin.

"Good morning," she said, trying not to sound

175

overly anxious or friendly. The woman behind the counter scarcely looked up. Her body language was an unspoken declaration that she wasn't going anywhere, she wasn't in a hurry, and she'd attend to customers when she was darn good and ready.

Ellen bit the inside of her lip and decided that patience was the only way to get what she was after.

Finishing her thumping with the rubber stamp, the woman finally pushed the pile of envelopes aside and turned in Ellen's direction.

"Next!" she called loudly, although Ellen was the only person on the far side of the counter.

"I hope you can help me," she said, instantly aware that an unmistakable note of desperation had crept into her voice.

"We'll see, won't we?" the woman replied.

Why not bite the bullet? She *was* desperate; there was no point in hiding it. "Look, it may sound crazy, but I've got to find the Von Ziegler estate. I know it's around here, but I'm not sure where. It's very important. Please help me."

"Against regulations," she said, folding her hands piously before her on the counter.

Something in the woman's gesture told Ellen the case wasn't quite closed. "I'm sure you're right," she said. "I wouldn't be doing this if it weren't so important. Isn't there anyone in town who can help me?"

The woman looked over one shoulder, then the other, and leaned across the counter.

"River Road. High stone wall. Iron gates with big lion heads in each of 'em. Can't miss 'em. But don't say who told you."

Ellen gave the woman's hands a grateful squeeze.

"I really appreciate this. Thank you so much!"

She was already out of town and on the way to the river when she began to consider the possible consequences. No one knew where she was or what she was doing. If she disappeared like the others, would anyone even think of looking for her in Rhinelander? Even if they did, the man at Rossler's Market wasn't likely to be much help. Neither would the woman in the post office. She scolded herself for being such a sissy. Furthermore, she had a decided advantage. Once she found this Von Ziegler character, she knew more about him than he did about her.

The high stone wall wasn't visible until it emerged from the trees surrounding the estate and ran along the road a short distance from the main gate. Ellen was so deep in thought, she nearly drove right past it. Then something in her peripheral vision made her slam on the brakes. She came to a full stop opposite the rusted, iron gates.

She stared at them in disbelief. This was something she hadn't counted on, let alone even thought of. The gates were held shut with two thick metal chains, bound top and bottom and secured with a formidable-looking padlock.

For several minutes, she sat quite still, staring at the gates. Was it possible that the padlocks might actually be loose? She'd come this far, there was certainly no reason not to cross the road and see for herself.

Leaving the car door partially open, she climbed out, not wishing to make the slightest sound to alert Von Ziegler that a stranger approached his property.

There were no cars in sight as she ran to the far side

and made her way to the tall iron gates. Heart racing with unexplained fear, she felt her mouth go dry.

Once close enough to get a better look, she was surprised that the clasps on the padlocks were not securely in place. All she had to do was remove the locks, pull the chain through the gate and she'd be inside. Her heart beat even faster.

"Stop! Stop right now or I'll turn you over to the police!"

Nineteen

Horst had leveled his gun directly at the woman fumbling around outside the gate. He sat on the ground behind a convenient copse of low pines that grew near the edge of the drive. They worked as effectively as though he planted them himself. It was a perfect vantage point to observe nosy creatures trying to spy on his property.

His finger began a slow squeeze on the trigger.

"Stop! Stop right now or I'll turn you over to the police!"

It was Hans in a rare display of machismo.

The prying bitch at the gate must have heard him, too, because she turned on her heels and ran straight for her car. Predictably, she was overzealous with the ignition. Her engine whined petulantly before she got herself together and sped off down the road. It was the sort of thing Horst loved to watch, and he would have been enjoying himself enormously if he weren't so furious with Hans.

He'd make him pay for this. Dearly.

Horst was planning a surprise for that feisty Felidia. Hans would help him carry it out. He would plead and complain and beg Horst not to do it, but the surprise would be good for both of them. Just in case either of them had any doubts as to who had the upper hand around here.

Expecting to be overtaken at any moment, Ellen sped along the narrow, winding road. She'd gone at least half a mile before she dared risk a glance in the rearview mirror. No one followed, but her foot sat heavily on the pedal. What a fool she'd been to attempt an undertaking like this completely on her own. Most of the time she was pretty fearless, but fearlessness was one thing; stupidity was quite another.

The situation would require the collaboration of many minds if they hoped to outwit this Von Ziegler character. They would have to move swiftly and carefully.

The name of Jim Sweeney led the list of her potentials.

Day and night had lost their boundaries and merged in a sensation of timeless gloom. Its only interruption came from the hours Horst spent with her, preparing his Felidia for her debut performance.

Judy had lost track of how long she'd been here. Sometimes she slept, sometimes she lay half-awake, half-asleep, wondering if she cared about anything anymore.

Poor Auntie. She must be sick with worry by now. At least she cared about that.

She was dozing when she heard footsteps on the stone floor. A heavy door swung open, allowing a shaft of light to pass through the bars and enter the cell. Hans was carrying a flat metal plate.

Was this breakfast, lunch, or dinner? It didn't really matter. She'd eaten almost nothing and realized she was starting to feel hungry for the first time since her capture. Hans slid the metal dish through the bars. There was no fork, no spoon. Just a single dish on the bare stone floor.

He watched her sadly as she assumed a position on all fours, then lowered her head so she could lap up the contents of the dish.

It was a stew of some kind.

Judy chased a piece of boiled potato around the dish until she captured it between her teeth and swallowed it almost whole. It wasn't long before she licked the plate completely clean.

When Hans leaned toward her to remove the dish, her eyes widened in horror.

"Where did you get that?" she demanded, pointing at the shirt that hung around him in loose folds. It wasn't until he moved toward her that the name *Bud,* embroidered in red just above the right breast pocket, came into view.

Hans simply stared back at her, looking wretched.

"He didn't! Promise me he didn't. No human being could do a thing as awful as that!" She began to scream and pound the bars with her fists, then gagged convulsively.

Hans watched like a forlorn child while she threw up everything she'd eaten in the corner of her cell.

* * *

He was off duty and heading for his car when Ellen Wallace took him by surprise in the parking lot. He already knew Bud Mosher's station hadn't opened that day. He'd tried to reach him by phone and had driven over in the cruiser on his lunch hour.

"Where's your car?" Jim Sweeney asked. He didn't intend to tell her about the day the two of them had borrowed the phone company van and paid an unofficial visit on Von Ziegler. Deep inside, a suspicion gnawed at him that Bud had gone freelance and made a return trip on his own. The look on Ellen's face only served to underscore what he was also feeling.

Jim lowered himself into the passenger seat and pulled a notepad from the pocket of his shirt.

"I'm miles away from doing this by the book, so you've got to help me."

"Fire away."

"What did Judy know about this Von Ziegler guy?"

"What did you tell her?"

"Nothing that isn't common knowledge around here."

"When she paid him that first visit, she said he was timid, not very sure of himself. She said she felt kind of sorry for him."

"That checks."

"With what?"

"What else?"

Ellen watched Jim scribble in the little book, but from where she sat she couldn't make out any of the writing. "Apparently, it was his brother who continued the family circus tradition. I think she said they were twins."

"Von Ziegler?"

"The first time she went there, Judy spent the afternoon with Hans, I think she said his name was."

Sweeney continued to scribble in his book, then paused for a moment and chewed on the end of his ballpoint pen. He was thinking about the afternoon he and Bud had surprised him with their phone-repair act. The man Ellen described was certainly the same guy they'd dealt with. There was no sign of any twin brother around, but in a place that size, he could have been anywhere.

"How many times was she there?"

"I'm not sure. A couple, I think." She turned in her seat to face him directly. "I feel so responsible for all of this. I tried to explain to her that these people had always been considered off-limits around here. But she was determined to meet them. You know that crazy notion she had about joining a circus? I guess I didn't take it seriously enough."

"She's a big girl, Miz Wallace. If she got it in her head to do something, I don't think you or anyone else could have stopped her. I had a little taste of that myself once."

"Then what do you propose we do?"

It was more a demand than a question, and Jim wished he had the answer. "Well, for one thing, we can't just go barging in there."

"Why not?"

"Because, if she is there, and we don't know that for sure, this Von Ziegler guy isn't going to thank us for stopping by and show us right to the place where she is."

Ellen stared out the car window. For the first time, she felt her eyes begin to well with tears. Up till now, she'd been too busy to cry. The hopelessness of the situation had finally gotten to her. She began to think about Harry. Maybe the two of them could get onto the Von Ziegler estate and do their own detective work.

"Forget it!" Jim Sweeney snapped.

Not bad, for a young guy, she thought. He read my mind and he was right. That doesn't mean I have to take his advice. Right now, more than anything, she wanted to be alone. She needed time to think.

"I hear you," she said. "And I have a restaurant to run. It's almost happy hour and Harry hates tending bar."

He knew she'd hoped to get more from him and he'd disappointed her. He also knew he couldn't tell her what else he knew. Besides, the day he played telephone man had yielded nothing substantial or he'd have been back there like a shot.

This time, Jim turned to face Ellen. "Luckily, we live in a place where there's almost zero crime — on a felony basis, that is. Read the police blotter in the *Ruttenburg Courier,* if you don't believe me. "Breaking and entering, noise complaints, illegal fireworks, stolen bicycle, suspicious loitering, driving while intoxicated. Very, very few kidnap cases, you'll discover." The look on Ellen's face told him she wished he'd stop trying to make sense and figure out a way to do what had to be done. "Suppose I go to the sheriff and tell him what I know you want me to tell him. First, he'd look at me like I was nuts, then he'd shove me out the door, and then I'd be back at the police academy to start all over again."

"We do what we have to do," she stated flatly and

started the car. "Let me know what you find out."

Sweeney jumped from the car, gave the door a slam, and waved to Ellen as she drove off.

Everything she said was true. He didn't know what to do about it.

Later that evening, Jim Sweeney and his brother, Law, decided to drop by the Rathskeller for a beer. They'd already killed a six-pack between them on the front porch after supper while Jim confessed his private escapade with Bud Mosher.

At first, Law couldn't believe he'd done it. Not that he'd taken it upon himself to crash the Von Ziegler estate, but that he'd gone with Mosher. What the hell ever happened to family loyalty, he wanted to know.

It took a lot of explaining, but Law finally got the point. If anything really went wrong, somebody had to be left at home to keep things on track. If it went wrong on a departmental level, he wanted his brother to be squeaky clean.

That's my version of family loyalty, Jim informed him.

The bar at the Rathskeller was half full when they got there. Ellen rushed over the minute they came through the door.

"Any word yet from Bud Mosher?" Jim asked, trying to sound as though the question hadn't been already answered in his own mind.

Ellen shook her head.

There was a vacant space at one end of the bar and

Law Sweeney was heading for it. Jim and Ellen were right behind him.

He pushed the bar stool toward the wall and leaned against it. This way, he knew there wouldn't be anyone eavesdropping behind him.

"We found Judy's bike in the creek, but there was no sign of her anywhere around. The next day we had the dogs out sniffing around and all they found were a couple of dead birds. They dragged the creek about five miles in both directions. Nothing."

"I know where she is," Ellen insisted. "Somebody has to go there and find out what happened."

"Go where?"

"To the Von Ziegler place over in Rhinelander. That's where she went, I know it. She went to meet the twin brother, the one who was with the circus, and she never came back."

"She told you that?"

For the first time, Ellen seemed to lose confidence in her argument. "Well, not exactly."

"What did she tell you?"

Ellen looked from Law to Jim and back again. "Jim and I discussed all of this before. Ask him, if you don't believe me."

When he spoke again, his voice was so low it was scarcely audible. "We've been there already, Miz Wallace."

Again, her eyes went from one to the other, searching for more information. "And?"

"And, nothing. Just this bland kind of guy. No sign of circus performers."

She stared accusingly at Jim. "Why didn't you tell me this?"

"Sorry, ma'am. Not allowed to talk about certain things." He got out of that one easier than he expected.

Ellen looked crestfallen. "What about Bud Mosher?"

"It'll be pretty hard down at the station house to convince 'em those two didn't hightail it out of here together. Give 'em a couple of weeks at the most. They'll be back here as Mr. and Mrs., happy as two pigs in shit."

If dirty looks were lethal weapons, Law Sweeney would have been lying dead on the floor. Ellen was so furious she couldn't speak.

It was Jim who came to the rescue. "Law didn't mean that like it sounded, Miz Wallace."

"And I suppose Kathy Kraus was the maid of honor, is that what you're trying to tell me?"

Law shrugged. "I bet you're not far off the mark."

She started to speak, but nothing came out. No wonder Judy was so anxious to leave this town. Did anyone have a brain in their head? First Kathy Kraus disappeared. Then Judy disappeared. Now Bud Mosher was missing, and all they could hear were wedding bells? Dear God, she thought. I'm right back where I started from.

They were halfway back to the center of Ruttenburg before either of them spoke.

"You were too rough on her," Jim said finally.

"I didn't want her expecting more than we can deliver."

"What the hell can we deliver? I saw this guy, Law.

He's a real wimp. Mid to late fifties. Walks around like he's a hundred. No balls."

"Then it's the brother we're looking for, right?"

"Maybe he's up there someplace. He didn't show his face while Bud and I were there."

"Is there a circus playing anywhere around?"

"Not since we were in grammar school."

"That was a carnival."

"Oh, yeah. And some kid fell out of the ferris wheel."

"Remember that? The old guy who ran the *Ruttenburg Courier* was all pissed off about safety and the sleaze bags that ran those things. Christ, he ran editorials about that for a year."

"And we never had another carnival, did we?"

Law Sweeney didn't answer. He simply stared into the dark night, beyond the headlights of his car. "What was that guy's name?" he asked finally.

Jim thought for a minute. "McSomething. McBride, I think it was. That fat woman who works in the library is his daughter."

"Do you think he's still alive?"

"Who knows? If he is, he's pretty old."

"Tomorrow, you and I are going to find out."

They drove the rest of the way home in silence. Law Sweeney was wearing an expression Jim had long since learned to respect if he didn't want his head chewed off.

His brother was hatching a plan. He'd find out about it soon enough, provided he didn't ask questions while Law was thinking.

Twenty

The Ruttenburg Public Library started off in life as a Methodist church. It was small and compact, like almost every other building in town designated to accommodate its tiny population. But after World War II when everyone was feeling prosperous, the Methodists decided to move their place of worship out of the center of town and closer to the part of town where a new community seemed to spring up overnight.

The public library lost part of its roof in a bad storm a week before the Methodists consecrated their new church and the books were all moved to the old one for safekeeping. It wasn't much later that the books discovered this was their permanent home.

Miriam McBride got her first job there right after college and she'd been town librarian ever since. Her two-hundred-pound frame filled the space behind the desk where she sat when Law and Jim Sweeney entered the following morning. She eyed them suspiciously as they approached. Two uniformed policemen didn't fit the profile of early-morning borrowers.

"Miz McBride?" Law asked, approaching the desk. "I'm Law Sweeney. Remember me? This is Jim, my brother."

She continued to regard them with a look that said she was keeping her distance. "Sweeney? Sweeney? Not the Hellraiser Sweeneys?"

Jim did an embarrassed shuffle in front of the desk and lowered his head. "I'm afraid so, ma'am. But we don't do that stuff anymore."

"I should hope not!" she sniffed. She took a closer look at Jim, then at Law. "I remember you two. Cops, huh? It's a wonder the pair of you aren't in jail yourselves!"

"That's right, ma'am," Law laughed. "You might say we got religion."

"Just in the nick of time," Jim smiled. "Now we're keeping the town of Ruttenburg safe for law-abiding citizens like yourself. In fact, folks call us Law and Order."

Miriam McBride shook her head in dismay. "I don't get around much like I did when you boys were in high school. Had my old dad to look after. Now he's gone and I still don't do much."

Law's eyes gave a quick glance in Jim's direction, but his younger brother had already taken the bit. "Miz McBride, I hope that doesn't mean . . ."

Instantly, she caught his drift and laughed. "Heavens, no. Gone. Not dead, if that's what you're driving at."

The Sweeneys let out simultaneous sighs of relief. "Well, that's good news, isn't it?" Law smiled over at Jim.

"Where's he at these days, Miz McBride?" Law inquired.

"Sunshine Hill Nursing Home. You boys know the place, don't you?"

"Right. Our greataunt Kay was there for six months before she died. Nice place."

"I bet he could use a couple of visitors, every once in a while. I sure have fond memories of your old dad when he was running the town paper. In fact, I used to deliver the *Courier* when I was in grammar school. Jim and I were talking about it just last night."

It was Jim's turn to carry the ball. "What d'you think, Miz McBride? Would it be okay if Law and I visited your father some day this week?"

It took her a long time to answer. "I don't know if it'd be much worth your while. He's in and out."

The Sweeneys looked at each other then back at Miriam McBride. "By 'out,' you mean . . . ?" Law queried.

"Good days and bad. It's the luck of the draw. I kept him home with me until finally it got to be too much."

"I see," Law answered, then smiled brightly. "But maybe it would give him a lift to see one of his old paperboys again. What do you think?"

"It's up to you. But don't expect much."

The lobby of the Sunshine Hill Nursing Home was lined with wheelchair patients sitting next to sofas and armchairs where friends and family members kept a regular, daily vigil.

The Sweeneys had decided to pay their call right

191

after lunch, before nap time, if that was part of old McBride's usual routine. On the drive over, they figured he had to be over ninety by now. They weren't at all sure what they were going to find.

A receptionist in the lobby told them that McBride's room was number 130 in the Richmond wing, then pointed to the elevator serving that part of the building.

As it rose toward their destination, it stopped halfway while three wheelchair-driven residents got on, returning to their rooms from an early afternoon social hour. They nodded and smiled at the Sweeneys, who nodded and smiled back.

"I'll bet some of those nighttime people have been caught stealing again," one resident said to another, in the kind of voice the hard-of-hearing use while talking to each other.

Jim wanted to reassure them that as far as he knew, their possessions were still safe, but the elevator doors opened again and the trio rolled out.

When they reached room 130, the cadaverous-looking man in the bed by the windows was sound asleep, his mouth wide open. It was only the raspy snoring sound he was making that assured them he was still alive.

"Now what?" Jim inquired of his brother. "Think we should wake him?"

"Shit," mumbled Law only slightly under his breath. "We could be here all afternoon." He moved a little closer to the bed. "It's sure a bitch to get old. I'd never have recognized this guy."

There was an empty bed on the other side of the room and Jim sat on its edge. "Say his name. See what happens."

First, Law took a deep breath, then cleared his throat. "Okay. Um, Mr. McBride," he said, not wanting to frighten the old man if he should wake with a start. Nothing happened. "Mr. McBride," louder this time, but still no response from the sleeping man. He looked at Jim helplessly. Jim gave him an encouraging nod. He should try it again. "Mr. McBride!" he shouted, then wished he had been just a bit more gentle.

The last thing he wanted to do was to frighten the old guy and wreck any chance they might have had to get him to reminisce about the past. Without warning, a voice came from the hallway just outside the room.

"Who the hell is making all that racket?"

The Sweeneys turned in unison to see a bespectacled, bald-headed man also in a wheelchair propelling himself through the door. He eyed the two with a mixture of curiosity, welcome, and weariness. Jim was the first to speak as he leapt from the edge of the empty bed. "Sorry, sir. We came to see Mr. McBride here. Unfortunately, he's sound asleep."

"Like hell he is," said the man in the wheelchair.

The Sweeneys exchanged a look. Was the sleeping man unconscious?

Then the man in the wheelchair gave off a laugh that should have wakened the dead. "What do you two buggers want? I'm McBride, for crissake."

The two were instantly on their feet, coming toward him. "Mr. McBride," Law said, smiling broadly and extending his hand in greeting. "I'm Law Sweeney, remember me? I used to deliver papers for you when I was a kid. This is my brother, Jim."

McBride gave him a long look. "Vaguely, vaguely," he replied finally. Then he looked at Jim. "Who's under arrest?"

"Nobody. Yet."

"Too bad. I can think of a couple of people I wouldn't mind seeing locked up in the slammer."

Law looked around the room, then back at McBride. "Is there a place we can talk, privately?"

"What's wrong with this?"

Law jerked his head in the direction of McBride's sleeping roommate.

Again came a laugh that could have cracked plaster. "He's deaf as a fence post. It doesn't get much more 'private' than this."

McBride rolled his chair next to the empty bed and indicated that the Sweeneys should join him in that part of the room he called his own.

"I hope you can help us," Law began.

McBride's eyes twinkled and he smiled. "All depends."

"My brother and I were talking about that carnival years ago when the kid fell out of the ferris wheel. Do you remember that?"

"I can't remember who I talked to five minutes ago. That's the trouble with living too long."

Both Sweeneys nodded in sympathy. They should have expected this. Miriam McBride had warned them, but they'd decided to try anyway.

"Well, you're looking good, Mr. McBride," Jim offered, wondering how long they'd have to make small talk before they admitted defeat and took their leave.

"I look good and I can't remember for shit. Except for things that happened thirty, forty years ago. Then I can tell you everything. Care to hear the Gettysburg Address? I learned that in high school."

Law shot a look at his brother that told him the interview wasn't over yet.

"Then I bet you do remember that carnival!"

"Sure I do. I wrote editorials in the paper about those people all summer long. That's the trouble, those carnival people aren't accountable to anyone. They come into town, they set up, they're there for a couple of weeks, and they're gone. Try and find 'em if they've skipped out on their bills or someone gets hurt . . ." His voice trailed off and it was clear his mind had drifted back to an issue he'd cared deeply about many years before.

"Do you remember the Circus Von Ziegler, Mr. McBride?"

It took a long time for his focus to return to the younger man who stood leaning against his bed.

"Von Ziegler?" He looked puzzled.

"You knew them, I'm sure. They bought that big place over in Rhinelander. They were very famous, once."

From the look on his face, they were sure they'd drawn a blank. He simply stared through the window, for a long while, saying nothing. His daughter had told them, "He comes and goes." He seemed to have left them and was now somewhere miles away. Neither Sweeney knew what to say or just what to do next.

It was McBride himself who finally broke the silence.

"God Almight! What the hell's the matter with me? Of course I remember them. That's just my point. They had that terrible accident, mauled to death in the ring, they were. And who's responsible? Who the hell knows? Somebody had to be pretty careless when two people like that are killed by one of their own animals. Their son was only a kid at the time. Went off the deep end. In fact, I think he was put away for a while."

"Which one?"

"One what?"

"Which son?"

"I forget the kid's name. Never mind, it doesn't matter, there was only one."

"I thought there were twins."

"Well, you thought wrong. Listen, my friend, I knew all about this. I used that story as background when I wrote those articles about the carnival accident." McBride's tone of voice turned unexpectedly belligerent, as though his professional credentials had been suddenly challenged.

"You can take my word for it. There weren't any twins. When the boy got out of the funny farm, he moved back to the family place in Rhinelander. People thought he'd want to sell it and get the hell out of there. Had to be filled with terrible memories. Last I heard he was still there. Nobody sees him much, I guess."

Before he could go on, a starched trim medication nurse pushed her wagon through the door. McBride's eyes lit up. "There she is, my little lamb." He turned to the Sweeneys. "Would you believe she's got two sons in high school? She looks like a little cheerleader, herself."

"How're you doing this afternoon, Bill?" she asked as if there were no one else in the room, while she wrapped a blood-pressure cuff around his arm.

"Always good, when you're around." He smiled at her in genuine appreciation. "Am I still alive?" he asked as she made her notes in his chart.

"You'll outlive us all," she laughed, then handed him a small cup containing two pills.

"Give me a glass of water," he ordered Jim, who was closest to the table beside his bed.

McBride's roommate was still sleeping and the medication nurse yelled in his ear. "John!"

The rhythmic snores became snorts and his eyes popped open. "Time for your pills, John!" she yelled again.

"What?"

"Pills!" she shouted, holding the small cup in front of his face so he could see it.

"Oh. Is it time for my pills?"

"That's right, John," she yelled again.

"Pills, is it?"

The Sweeneys pretended not to notice the scene on the other side of the room.

"What'd I tell you?" McBride demanded. "Deaf as a fence post!"

As the medication nurse pushed her cart out the door, McBride called after her. "Come on back here when you're done. I want to hear how those kids made out." She smiled and nodded back over her shoulder as she wrestled the cart around the corner and disappeared. "Two boys on the Ruttenburg team this fall. Nothing like the team they had in the early

197

Fifties. State champions in Fifty-one. Lost only one game in Fifty-two, but that was enough to lose the championship."

It was time to get the conversation back to where they started, Law Sweeney had decided. With a ninety-year-old man, you never knew what might happen next.

"We'd better be going, Mr. McBride," Law said in an attempt to get the old man's attention. "But I'd like to ask you something else."

Suddenly, Bill McBride looked exhausted. He had slumped in the chair and his chin was resting on his chest. It took great effort for him to raise his head. He looked at Jim Sweeney as though to say, "See if you can get this guy out of here."

Just then, another nurse bustled through the door. "Hi, Bill," she greeted him gaily. "Had your medication yet this afternoon?"

McBride stared at her blankly. "My what?"

"Your pills. Your saltpeter."

It took a moment, but once again came the laugh that seemed to come from somewhere in another lifetime. It was over almost as fast as it came and McBride was very quiet. "My pills? I don't know." He turned to Law Sweeney. "Did you see anyone give me my pills?"

Twenty-one

Horst stood at the window staring across the drive, over the treetops that surrounded the estate as far as the eye could see. Something had to be done about Hans. He had known it since they were children.

Hans could not be trusted. It was time to face the undeniable fact that Hans would have to be destroyed. He left the window and began to pace the room. When they were children, it was easy to ignore him. He wanted none of the things Horst did and he was no genuine threat. It was only as he grew older that Hans had become a problem.

Predictably, Hans was his mother's favorite. While Klaus Von Ziegler gave lip service to the pride he took in Horst and the extraordinary bravery his young son demonstrated in the circus ring, Horst believed that he, too, harbored a secret preference for the shy and fearful Hans.

Hans would never outshine his father in the ring. Hans would never mesmerize the audience with heart-stopping feats of skill and daring. Hans hated the circus ring. He much preferred the life they shared as a family when the circus moved from one town to another.

Once or twice, Horst had ridden the back of his father's Felidia at the head of the circus parade. It was only for a minute or so each time, but it was the thrill of Horst's young life. Hans would have been too frightened. In fact, he would have cried. All of them knew it and his father never invited Hans to take part. The danger and the excitement of the ring were not for timid souls. Hans knew his place and never asked for more.

That was his problem. He asked too little from life. Furthermore, he knew too much. He would have to be destroyed.

But how? And when?

His own Felidia preferred Hans to Horst and it was painful to know that, too. Eventually, she would come to love him more, and this time he would be more careful. There would be no surprises. No last-minute change in plan that would kill his dear Felidia.

The searing memory caused a knot to form at the base of his skull. The beautiful and graceful Ilse dragged across the ring by the back of her neck by that snarling, drooling lioness. Klaus was bleeding to death close-by, but Ilse was not to have been in the ring at all. He had arranged everything so carefully and at the last minute it went all wrong!

That morning, Hans had complained of fierce stomach cramps. He had vomited all night and the morning brought no relief. Ilse was to fetch medication for the boy while Klaus gave the animals a work-out before the evening performance. Under normal conditions, Hans fed the animals, but he'd been feeling poorly for several days and Horst insisted he take over the chores until Hans was feeling better. As the days went on, Hans felt worse and worse. He was scarcely able to get out of bed at all.

Horst knew the routine. It wasn't necessary to tell him what to do at feeding time. He went about his chores with a diligence and determination that surprised Klaus and Ilse. He had it down cold.

No one discovered Felidia had not been fed since Hans became ill.

Before Ilse left the campgrounds to get the medicine for Hans, she stopped to watch Horst prepare the animals' morning meal. She worried about him. He hadn't been feeling well either. Perhaps it was time for all of them to stop for a while and take a vacation. She planned to discuss it with Klaus as soon as she returned.

Horst was slicing pieces of cooked liver into the dish when his knife slipped and tore a nasty gash in his thumb. He screamed in pain, but his mother wasn't there. Blood dripped into the bowl used only for Felidia. He watched one drip follow another until a puddle of bright crimson filled the indentation at the bottom of the bowl. How long would it take for the flow to cease? He began to worry. What if he had cut an artery by mistake? Horst would be the one who would bleed to death with no one to come and rescue him.

He looked about and found a discarded rag nearby. He wrapped the thumb, ladled food into the bowl, and brought it to his father's precious Felidia.

Then he returned to his cot in one of the wagons and waited.

He was sleeping when the horrendous screams awakened him. For a long while, he lay perfectly still and listened.

Suddenly, new screams assaulted his ears. Someone had entered the ring with Klaus. Someone else had been attacked.

Drenched with sweat, Horst sprang from his cot and dashed for the main circus tent. It was nearly dark inside. Only a dim worklight illuminated the center ring. Horst dashed down the aisle, and when he reached the caged area inside the center ring, his father already lay in a bloody heap off to one side.

His throat was an open gorge of moist, ragged flesh, the face so badly clawed its features were no longer distinguishable. A chewed arm dangled indifferently from its socket and hung across the torso.

But the sight that froze Horst Von Ziegler to the spot where he stood was the lifeless body of his beloved mother being dragged about the ring by the flesh-crazed lioness.

This was never meant to happen! Not Ilse. Not his adored mother!

For years, he had been plotting some way to rid them of the tyranny of a father who insisted on being at the center of the spotlight. Horst would never achieve his rightful place as long as Klaus continued to dominate their lives.

But his plan included Ilse. His mother was to star with him in the center ring. Two generations of Von Zieglers, defying the beasts of the jungle. Together they would triumph in a way Klaus had never imagined.

What had gone wrong? Why was she there? Why was this happening?

He had to do something before it was too late.

His father kept a loaded gun in his dressing room. Horst ran back up the aisle of the tent, praying that the door to the dressing-room trailer hadn't been locked.

It wasn't. He burst inside and yanked open the drawer of the table where neat rows of greasepaint and pots of rouge waited in orderly fashion for the evening to begin.

The gun was there, just as it had been for as long as he could remember. Horst had been allowed to shoot when they traveled one summer in Africa. He could only hope that the weapon would at least stun, if not kill, the beast who was murdering his mother.

Back into the tent he flew. The moment he was close enough, he took aim. He fired once, twice, three times. The beast had opened its mouth and dropped Ilse into a pile of straw at one side of the ring. Rivulets of blood dyed its flaxen color almost instantly around the spot where she lay.

Sounds of gunshots brought other members of the circus family scurrying from all directions.

Hans came, too.

He had seen it all.

The years in the private hospital were expensive. Hans had wanted to sell the estate, but where else could Horst have captured and trained his cats?

The new act would be ready soon.

Of course, Hans would try to prevent him from advertising the triumphant return of the Circus Von Ziegler. Yet once Hans was disposed of, he could do things his own way.

That was how it should have been once Klaus was dead, but everything had gone wrong. Horst had waited years for this moment. He wasn't going to let Hans stop him now.

First, he must put an end to the love affair between Hans and his Felidia. It was only in Hans's mind, of course, but Horst knew he loved her just the same. And if it ever came to a choice of Hans or Horst, he knew Hans would win out.

A diabolical plan was taking shape at the back of his mind, but from the moment he had begun to think about the day Klaus and Ilse were mauled to death, his skull began to throb with splintering pain.

If he could rest for a while, he would be able to think more clearly later.

Somewhere down the dark passageway, a door opened. Judy listened intently. She heard footsteps making their way toward her.

She saw the silhouette and knew immediately it was Hans. He held something before him, carrying it with both hands. He set it on the floor just outside the door of Judy's cell.

Judy clung to the bars and pressed her face against them.

"Please, Hans," she begged in a voice that was scarcely audible. "You're the only one who can help me. Please? I'm afraid he's going to kill me."

"He loves you," was his only reply as he removed a heavy clip from his pocket and inserted one of its keys into the lock. It clicked and he pulled the door toward him. With one foot, he slid the basket he'd been carrying inside the cell, then pushed the door and locked it shut.

She stared at the basket on the floor. "What is this?" she demanded.

"Horst made me do it, Felidia. I'm very frightened. It's me he wants to kill."

A bare electric bulb at the end of a cord swung to and fro in the draft from the open door at the end of the passage. Judy stared at the basket; its contents were obscured by a torn piece of cloth thrown over the top.

"Horst says this is what happens when people butt in where they don't belong. I'm afraid I must go. I'm not feeling very well."

He left the light burning and slowly made his way down the passage.

She heard the door bang shut, and for a long while she sat, staring at the basket on the floor in front of her. Somewhere, deep within, she knew not to lift the cloth that kept its contents from plain view. Horst was playing psychological war games and she had to keep herself protected.

Yet she would have no idea how escalated the war had become until she saw what weapons he was using. One of those weapons was in the basket sitting before her.

More than an hour passed before she decided it was better to confront the enemy face-to-face.

She lifted a corner of the cloth, but the shadow it

cast made it difficult to see inside. Finally, with a resolute yank, she pulled the cloth completely away. As she did so, the basket toppled over and its contents rolled across the floor of her cell. It came to rest in the corner.

When she peered into the darkness, the two dead eyes of Bud Mosher's severed head stared back at her.

Judy screamed and screamed. She ran to the far side of the cell and clung to the bars. She screamed again and again until her throat felt as though a burning coal were embedded there. She knew it was useless, but she screamed anyway. It was all she could do to help rid herself of the hideous image that had seared its way into her brain.

Horst's warning rang in her ears. "This is what happens when people butt in where they don't belong." She had "butted in," too, hadn't she?

Would this be her fate, as well?

Twenty-two

Sometime during the night, Judy had placed the empty basket over Bud's head in the corner of her cell.

She couldn't see it, but she knew it was there.

Later, Horst appeared outside the cell, unlocked the door, and led her upstairs to continue her "training." She had done extremely well, he told her. He was so pleased he was contemplating a sneak preview of the Circus Von Ziegler.

It might happen any day now.

Did he actually intend to invite an audience to the estate to watch his "cats" perform, she wondered? Was Horst so completely removed from reality he didn't comprehend that the very event he was preparing would mean the end of his lunatic existence?

Horst's mad scheme was all she had to keep her from losing her mind.

As usual, she was not allowed to speak, but once they entered the ring, Judy encouraged him with new energy she brought to her performance. When their eyes met, she transmitted an unmistakable message that said, "See how well I can do? Watch this! And this!"

Horst was deliriously happy. He hadn't felt so exhilarated since he'd been permitted to ride his father's favorite lioness so many years before. Things were going very well.

Furthermore, Hans was so intimidated by him, he scarcely appeared at all anymore.

Very soon the Circus Von Ziegler would make its triumphal return.

It was Horst who now brought Judy her daily rations. She couldn't remember when she'd last been visited by Hans. Sometimes at night she'd wake and find Horst seated next to her cage, peering at her through the darkness.

"You're mine, Felidia," he would repeat again and again. "I chose you. The others simply can't compare. You are my Felidia and I will never let you go."

Judy pretended to be sleeping on the nights when this occurred. She fought to obliterate the sound of his voice. What still kept her sane was a desperate determination to escape. She fought to retain the belief it was still possible. He had broken the others. She must not let it happen to her.

She found herself wondering about Kathy Kraus. What had become of her? Was she alive or dead? Judy had lost all sense of time. How many days had passed since she discovered poor Kathy tethered at the wrists and dangling from a hook in the ceiling?

And Bud. Poor Bud. He had tried to rescue her and was murdered instead. Her stomach convulsed. The stewed meat Hans had fed her was the memory that did it.

No! If she thought about any of it for very long, Horst would break her, too. She had to hang on, focus on getting out of there. Otherwise, she'd be lost forever.

"Come, Felidia. I have a surprise for you!"

Horst was outside the cage with his set of keys and a piece of dark-colored fabric slung over his shoulder. He led Judy through the gate and tied the piece of fabric securely over her eyes.

It was useless to protest. Besides, the centerpiece of Judy's game plan was to convince Horst that his every word was her command. Even without seeing him, she knew he was agitated about something. His hands were moist and trembling when he grasped her wrist and guided her up the stone steps from the basement to the upper house. He had a strange, musky odor when he approached once again to untie the blindfold.

Judy discovered herself next to the circus wagon he had earmarked for his precious Felidia, its iron gate hanging open. Without further ceremony, he pushed her inside and locked the gate. Once again came the ritual descent of the curtains, plunging her into almost-total darkness with a suffocating absence of air, as the wagon began its slow, squeaking roll.

Again came the predictable blare of the brass band, but this time there was something else. When the circus fanfare concluded, Judy thought she heard some kind of buzz, an electrical hum.

Without warning, the sound of a single voice

echoed off the walls and vaulted ceiling of the vast ballroom.

"Ladies and gentlemen and children of all ages. Welcome to an event long awaited in circus history! From the training camp in Rhinelander, New York, we proudly present Horst Von Ziegler, heir to the Circus Von Ziegler, so beloved for more than half a century!"

What happened next gave Judy the first glimmer of genuine hope she'd experienced since Horst had taken her captive.

Somewhere beyond her draped cage, a crowd "Ohhed," and applauded with approval.

The madman had done it! He'd actually invited an audience who could testify to the atrocities he'd performed.

Poor Horst. For an instant, she pitied him.

"In the center ring, the singular, the unique, that intrepid tamer of wild beasts, Horst Von Ziegler and his fabulous felines!"

Again another roar. This one more like a thunderclap than a round of applause.

He's actually done it, Judy thought, dizzy from a sense of unexpected freedom. But he was clever, this Horst, and she had to be careful. Even with an audience surrounding him, she wasn't sure what he might do to ensure that she didn't escape.

Cool it, she told herself. If he's crazy enough to bring an audience in here, he's crazy enough to do anything.

Again the deafening blare of brass. The drapes flew up and Judy's cage was flooded with blinding light. Her eyes had yet to adjust to the glare when

Horst unlocked the gate, yanked on the chain about her neck, and pulled her down the steps.

Just a few minutes more, she told herself; something was bound to happen. Someone in the crowd was sure to protest, and that was her first step to freedom.

But the crowd roared again. The sound reverberated in her head. With the handle of her chain in one hand, Horst saluted his fans with the other.

At last, Judy's vision cleared and she stared beyond the blast of light into the seats surrounding the center ring. They were empty. Not a soul occupied the rows of bleachers lining the walls.

Tears were insufficient to express the stunning sense of desolation that swept over her.

The other "cats" sat pertly on their stools, obediently awaiting Horst's command to perform.

His eyes shone like deranged beacons and his face glistened with sweat. The whip cracked again and again and he grunted unintelligibly as his "cats" leapt from one platform to another.

The grasp with which he held the lead fastened to the metal band around Judy's neck was firm and sure. With each successive crack, he jerked the chain until the skin beneath the collar felt like it had been rubbed completely raw — a sharp, stinging sensation that burned like a fiery necklace.

One look revealed that Horst was on another plane, reliving another time, another place.

All hope of immediate escape dashed, Judy realized that to defy him now was to invite physical and emotional punishment once Horst concluded the performance was over.

Could this be the return of the Circus Von Ziegler? Did he intend to go on forever performing this fantasy, this circus of his mind? If so, no one need ever know of the women he had captured and held prisoner in the dungeonlike cellar of the sprawling estate. No one came near the place. He'd seen to that.

As Horst led her about the ring, Judy suddenly found herself staring at one of the "cats" whimpering and fidgeting atop a nearby platform. Except for the tiny bit of animal skin that covered her loins and breasts, her skin was bare. Above the freckled breasts were swollen, pink welts where Horst's bullwhip had found its mark with deadly accuracy. But it was her back that had received most of the damage. Long ridges of folded, open flesh crisscrossed from her shoulders to her waist.

I'm next, Judy thought, unless I can outsmart him, and God knows when that will be. How do you outfox a fox?

The next yank on her chain nearly pulled her off her feet. She reeled, her head swam and her vision blurred, but a voice deep within told her she mustn't disappoint him. She was his prized Felidia, performing for an adoring audience that only Horst could see.

The whip snapped so close it sounded like a firecracker in her ear.

Dear God, get us out of here, she prayed without the slightest hope of being heard.

He drove along, the winding road looking for a spot to pull over and leave his car where it wouldn't

212

be noticed by anyone traveling in either direction. Jim Sweeney was out of uniform, dressed in the same clothes he'd worn when he and Bud Mosher made their visit to Von Ziegler in the guise of telephone repairmen. This time, his personal, snub-nosed .38 revolver was tucked inside his belt.

He scaled the stone wall protecting the property and picked his way through the woods until the massive structure came into view. Just looking at it gave him chills.

When he and Bud were here before, they came to the kitchen door. He opted for the same approach to keep Von Ziegler from getting suspicious.

It surprised him that the door was slightly ajar when he reached the house.

Jim peered into the room beyond. It was empty. He rapped quietly on the door, then stepped inside.

"Mr. Von Ziegler, sir?" he called, unsure what might happen next. No one answered. Jim fidgeted with the tool belt strapped at his waist. For a moment, he considered backing off and returning later — then he remembered Bud's insulting remark after they were here before. A *pussy* was something he'd never been and didn't plan to start now. Fuck it, he told himself. Go for it and work out the fine points later.

He moved quietly through the house. Its windows were heavily draped and the light was dim, yet its former splendor was still evident. In what had been a spectacular salon, its once-elegant furnishings were in desperate need of repair.

Stealthily and silently, he moved from room to room, never sure what he would discover or when

213

Von Ziegler might discover him. Unexpectedly, he found himself in a makeshift artist's studio. Beautiful, brightly rendered lions, tigers, panthers, and leopards were stacked against all four walls. He was amazed at how well painted they all were. Individually, they might have been worth thousands.

Turning, he spotted a large easel, in the center of the room, a dropcloth covering its canvas.

Idle curiosity more than anything prompted him to pull the cloth away, completely unprepared for what he found. Staring back was a beautiful young lioness, surrounded by a mane of glorious golden hair with the face of Judy McAuliffe.

A tidal wave of adrenaline flooded his veins. It took less than an instant to convince him that Von Ziegler was a some kind of psychopath, possibly dangerous and probably holding Judy prisoner within the confines of his vast estate.

He remembered how panicky Von Ziegler had become when Bud tried to open that cellar door. "Damn!" Jim exclaimed aloud. She was in that basement all along and they'd left her there.

It was more important than ever not to blow it. If Von Ziegler found him before he could locate Judy, he'd have a bitch of a time making his case. He was trespassing, without a warrant, and he knew it.

With catlike movements, Jim was retracing his steps when he first heard brassy music coming from the floor above. He froze, then listened. There it was again. It sounded like a circus band.

His mind began to race. Pure, gut-level instinct drove him toward the sound. Lions, tigers, panthers. It was starting to make sense in a nightmarish kind of way. He flew up the formal staircase leading to the ballroom.

The gruesome spectacle he witnessed was more sickening than anything he imagined.

Not more than fifteen feet away, a cluster of dazed, obviously beaten young women, many with open and ugly flesh wounds, sat perched on tiny platforms like tamed and broken beasts. Some wore furry little bikini costumes. Some were completely naked.

At the center of the ring, Von Ziegler cracked his whip. On a long tether, attached to a steel ring that encircled her neck, Judy McAuliffe pranced around its perimeter. She was dressed in a scanty loincloth and tiny halter. The harder Von Ziegler cracked his whip, the higher she would jump. Her bared flesh dripped with sweat.

Judy's breath was coming in ragged gasps; she didn't know how much longer she could continue this charade, before collapsing in total exhaustion.

"All right, freeze!" shouted a voice from somewhere among the tiers of empty seats.

She whirled about to see Jim Sweeney, his .38 revolver leveled at Horst.

Horst's hand was faster than the eye and the whip had already been unfurled. It coiled around Sweeney's wrist, tossing the weapon into the air.

Quick as a cat, he withdrew the length of cowhide and lashed out again. This time, the whip encircled Sweeney's throat. Horst stepped back and with a single, mighty yank pulled the younger man off his feet.

When he hit the hard oak floor, Sweeney was knocked cold.

Horst tugged on the whip, but all he could do was to pull Sweeney's unconscious body closer and closer to him. His face flushed with rage. He clenched his teeth and began to growl. Feverishly, he worked to free the whip from its tangled hold around Jim Sweeney's throat.

His "cats" were becoming agitated. Something had changed. Judy wasn't sure exactly what it was until suddenly, and without warning, one of them sprang from her platform with a wild shriek, landing full weight across Horst's back.

For a moment, he was stunned, then threw her off. But this action had galvanized the others. On some deep animal level, a signal had been given that the predator was now their victim.

One after the other they came, pouncing and attacking with the ferocity of jungle beasts. A caldron of violence was about to boil over.

Wild shrieks filled the air. They pounced on Horst. One bit his neck so deeply that blood spurted in her face. She reared back with bloodstained teeth, emitting a satisfied cry while another tore at his flesh. Still another dug fingers into his eyes.

His arms and legs flailed while they fought and scratched each other for more advantageous position. At last, a sea of crimson flowed from the mutilated body in the center ring.

Their rage appeased, the "cats" grew quiet. They formed a circle and hunched around the motionless body.

Lawrence Sweeney knew Jim was up to something, particularly since he refused to talk about it. He was sure it involved the town's three unofficially declared missing persons.

He'd driven up and down the road near the Von Ziegler estate at least five or six times before noticing Jim's car hidden in the trees. It didn't take a crystal ball to figure where he went.

By the time Law got himself onto the property and into the mansion, Jim had regained consciousness. Judy McAuliffe was still in shock. Luckily, there were several blankets in the trunk of his car.

Law wrapped Judy in one of them and Jim gave others to the "cats" who still remained naked.

For a long while, Judy stared blankly off into space, never uttering a sound. When they spoke to her, she wouldn't or couldn't answer. Then, quietly at first, she began to sob. Her body heaved and heaved again.

Putting a protective arm around her shoulder, Jim tried to dry her tears, but it was no use. Her body shook convulsively until she was left gasping for air. At last, she looked up, tears still flooding her eyes.

"He's dead," was all she could manage to say.

It had been his fear all along, once he found Judy alive, his hopes for Bud had been raised as well.

An inner voice he'd learned to trust told him this wasn't the time to discuss it. Between sobs, Judy informed them Kathy Kraus might still be alive, tied up in the basement.

Jim rushed for the cellar stairs while Law radioed for assistance. They would need more ambulances than the town could provide. Then he called the Rathskeller.

When Ellen answered, he told her to find some clothes for her niece and go bring them to the Von Ziegler estate.

Nothing Law or Jim Sweeney learned at the police academy prepared them for sorting out the physical and mental carnage that faced them that night.

Twenty-three

By the time Ellen and Harry arrived with Judy's clothes, the front lawn of the mansion looked like a field hospital. Judy stumbled down the drive, supported by her aunt on one side and her uncle on the other. As the trio approached the police cruiser, the Sweeney brothers were leaning on the hood.

Judy stopped for a moment and stared at Jim. "How did you know we were here?" she asked in a voice that was scarcely audible.

"Call it a lucky hunch," Jim replied cautiously. It was going to be hard telling Judy the full story, but there was plenty of time for that later. Besides, she deserved to know the truth.

As one of the ambulances was pulling away, Jim tried to hail it. He was sure they had room for one more.

"Oh, no you don't," Ellen informed him adamantly. "We'll drive this little lady to the hospital ourselves. She's not getting out of my sight for a minute!"

Kathy Kraus was unconscious but alive, trussed

up hand and foot, when Jim Sweeney found her in the basement. She was one of the first to be taken away in the convoy of ambulances rolling down Von Ziegler's drive. The triage team at St. Ursula's hospital five miles away marked her for a bed in Intensive Care, but they were ill-prepared to handle the parade of ambulances that continued to arrive, one after the other.

Many had to be redirected to facilities that were better equipped to handle the psychological trauma Von Ziegler had inflicted on his victims.

Law Sweeney still couldn't believe half the things he saw and heard that night. Stuff like this only happened in the movies. Certainly not in a God-forsaken corner of the world like theirs.

"Who'd have ever thought this weirdo would turn out to be so dangerous? And absolutely nuts!" Law exclaimed incredulously, staring at the taillights of a disappearing ambulance as it snaked its way down the drive.

Judy started to move away, then turned. "What about the other one?"

"There isn't another one," Jim told her. "When you're up to it, I'll stop by the Rathskeller and tell you the whole story. Believe me, we got it on good authority. There's only one. That's what made me decide to take another look. Only this time, I figured I'd better have Law along as backup."

Law continued to stare off into space. "Jesus," he whispered softly to himself.

By some perverted miracle, Von Ziegler was still clinging to life when they loaded him into one of the ambulances that converged on the property from miles around. If anyone asked him, Law would have to confess he hoped the guy wouldn't make it. Institutions for the criminally insane made him nervous. There was always the chance some do-gooder psychiatrist would decide he was ready to rejoin society five or ten years from now.

Then, they could just sit back and wait for the whole scenario to replay itself all over again.

Pray to God he dies before he gets to St. Ursula's, he told himself.

Beside him, his brother stood rooted to the spot, hands clasped firmly beneath his buttocks where he leaned against the car. Jim intended to stay right where he was until fully convinced that his hands had stopped shaking.

It was Jim Sweeney who had lifted the basket that covered Bud Mosher's severed head. And it was Jim Sweeney who had raised the lid of the food locker and discovered the frozen remains of Bud as well as of several unidentifiable females.

No one saw him run into the yard and vomit until there was nothing left. His stomach continued to heave long after it was empty and only drips of bile rose to moisten his bitter-tasting mouth.

What a pair of dumb smart-asses they'd been, plotting their telephone scam. He'd known enough not to tell Law about their plan when they hatched it. Law was such a straight arrow once he joined the force, it was like he'd gotten religion.

But Jim had known Bud would be up for it. Especially since he had the major hots for Judy McAuliffe. Christ, he thought, this is one I'm going to have to live with for the rest of my life.

At first, he didn't even hear his brother behind the wheel of the cruiser blowing the horn.

Law leaned across the seat. "Get in. We've still got work to do."

"I could use a drink," Jim said, giving a yank to the door on the passenger's side that could have pulled it from its hinges.

"Later," Law informed him. "First, we visit St. Ursula, then the station, then we have a drink or two, maybe."

Jim said nothing. He stared out the window all the way to the hospital. It was the kind of silence Law knew from the time they were kids. It was also the kind of silence he knew better than try to interrupt.

Some things, Law mused to himself, are better left alone.

Epilogue

In early September when the moon is full, it casts a light so bright one can almost read by it. It was that kind of moon illuminating the great stone mansion perched on the edge of a hill, high above the river.

On one of the upper floors, a window was open. Its tattered curtain floated on the breeze drifting upward from the river.

An eerie light bathed the imposing structure in an ethereal, ghostly glow.

If anyone had been standing in the drive and glanced upward, they might have sworn they saw the sparkle of something gold reflected in the moonlight. Too, they might have thought they caught a glimpse of crimson behind the curtain as it fluttered to and fro.

If anyone remained once the convoy of police and ambulances snaked their way down the drive and disappeared into the night, they might have had the disquieting sense that someone was up there, watching.

If one is fearful by nature, the imagination can play havoc with one's perception of reality.